TEMPTRESS OF ELDER HALLOW

Celestial Series Book Five

Lillith Carrie

LILLITH CARRIE PUBLISHING

Cover Design by Natasha Designs

Editing by Aimee Ferro Edits

Printed by Ingramspark

First edition, 2023.

www.lillithcarriepublishing.com

PROLOGUE

Pain and loss was something I would never grow accustomed to, even with so much of it befalling my family over the last decade. I couldn't come to terms with how easily it was for people to be torn from me when I least expected it.

The moment I felt the tether to my mother break, my heart was torn to pieces.

Running through the forest over fallen trees and broken branches, I tried to reach the others. For a year, my family had been helping my sister find a missing piece to some puzzle. I hadn't been privy to all the information, but Silas had made it clear I was more of an asset then the others had thought. He was the one who had insisted that I came on this mission, standing toe to toe with my brother and demanded my presence. I would aid him if my brother didn't want me around.

Even if that meant I had stayed at the cars from the moment we got here.

Things had been different since Cassie took over Asgard. Most of our family moved on to Asgard. However, I couldn't help but feel like my place in the pack wasn't needed as if I was meant for something so much more. Even if my wolf whined at the idea of us leaving my family home.

At the end of the day, I was nothing more than the Alpha's little brother who only survived as a child because his sister saved him.

Something I would forever be grateful for, but also something that left me completely confused growing up. I couldn't understand why Cassie had wanted to save me.

A fire crackled in the distance as tree branches danced with the glow of flames, falling to the ground one after the other. The burst of power from whatever my family faced had caused so much damage—a reckoning unlike anything I had ever seen.

"Lux!" I called, stepping from the trees into a brightly lit clearing. In its center was an old wooden cabin, flames reaching for the sky though the cabin didn't actually seem to catch a blaze. Magic must protect it, but the forest had been fair game.

"Lux!" I yelled as panic filled my chest. My eyes searched the surrounding area for my brother whose figure was currently the only one I couldn't really recognize.

With heavy smoke in the air, and the sounds of screaming and howls of injured wolves, it was hard to tell which direction to go into. Bodies of all sizes scattered around the ground, their agony resonating through the air.

As much as I wanted to stop and help them, I couldn't. The urgency to find my family was higher than the need to help others. Perhaps, that made me selfish but it didn't matter. At least not to me, not in that moment.

Shielding my eyes, I searched through the smoke and flames. I maneuvered around the crying figures of hunters and dead wolves who weren't part of my family's pack. My heart raced, my breath short and chest heavy—I simply prayed to the goddess none of the faces I saw would be of someone I knew.

I wasn't sure what the hell happened, but from the looks of it, shit didn't go as planned.

"Tate! Get out of here!" My father, Talon, yelled at me from across the clearing. My mother's fallen form in his arms caused the ache to hurt even more. I ran towards them hoping what I was seeing wasn't real.

"What happened?!" I screamed above the cries of others, dropping to my knees beside him. His eyes filled with tears as he shook his head, seemingly unable to formulate the right words.

"It doesn't matter. We have to be strong right now. Fate deemed it her time, and it won't be forever." Turning, his stern gaze captured my own as he let out a heavy breath. "Remember that...it won't be forever, Tate. We will see her again."

I wanted to fight against what he was saying, but I knew it was true. We would see her again, eventually, but it didn't make the pain hurt any less.

She will be waiting for me, I repeated in my head, trying to keep my heart together. "I need to find Pollux."

"No, you need to get out of here, Tate. Go back to the cars and get the fuck out of here."

Shaking my head, I tried to ignore the itch to help my father. My brother was the Alpha of the pack now, and our people needed him to guide them into the future. Making sure our Alpha was safe was the only priority I had.

"I can't...I have to find Pollux."

Rushing towards the cabin, I searched through thick smoke for the face I needed to see most. The burn at the back of my throat caused me to cough as I weaved in and out of debris towards the familiar voice of his beta. Their bodies came into view the moment I rounded the far side of the cabin, where they stood looking down at something at their feet.

"We have to get out of here," Sam, my brother's beta, called out as I approached the circle of people surrounding none other than my brother and the body of a woman.

"This wasn't supposed to happen..." Pollux's words fell short, my eyes cast towards the middle of the circle formed by my brothers pack members. Their eyes were glued to the middle-aged woman adorned with tattered clothing, scars, and soot upon her body. An angry gaze crossed his eyes as he sneered, looking up at those who surrounded him. "Who killed her!"

Silence. It was all that followed his question as if every single person was either too afraid to speak up or didn't actually know.

"I–I don't know," Sam finally replied. "There was so much light, and then the fire and smoke. I didn't see what happened until it all cleared."

My brother's eyes filled with anger and fell to the woman in his arms. I wasn't sure what was going through his head but as he laid her lifeless body on the ground—golden hair tattered with dirt and blood—I knew he would be out for revenge.

"It was Moria. That stupid fucking bitch did this! She betrayed us all!" Pollux roared, the rage of his hatred flowing through the pack link like a devastating fire threatening to burn us all. "I should have fucking known she would be here!"

"Alpha, there is nothing that can be done now. We have to go," Sam repeated, seriousness laced in his words.

"Where's the other woman?" Pollux seethed, glaring at his beta. "Where did she go?"

Sam's eyes widened as his mouth dropped open, shaking his head. "I don't know. The moment the light cleared, she was gone."

I wasn't sure who they were talking about, but by the desperate look that seemed to cross my brother's eyes, it was clear that he hadn't planned for this to happen. When we left the pack lands to come here, they acted as if this was going to be easy. As if whatever they were coming to do wasn't going to take long, but Silas had still insisted on back up.

Pollux hadn't thought it a good idea, at first.

My brother was notorious for being the best there was when it came to tracking supernaturals. He and my sister-in-law Trixie helped so many targeted by the human hunting organization Elite Humanity, but this was the first time one of his operations had gone south.

Dead hunters and shifters littered the ground. A sight forever imprinted in my mind no matter how hard I tried to forget it. Everywhere I looked, signs of the battle that had taken place surrounded me.

No longer would saving people be easy. This event would attract more attention from Elite Humanity, and with the losses we took today that itself was going to be problematic for us.

"We have to go."

I had remained silent since I arrived, but when I spoke all eyes turned to me. I was the baby of the family—the child treasured above all others by a queen who saw greatness in my future. A treasure my brother was sworn to protect.

"What are you doing out here?" Pollux snapped, standing to his feet and stepping towards me. "You were supposed to wait in the car."

I rolled my eyes, crossing my arms over my chest. "With an explosion that big? Yeah, that wasn't going to happen."

He didn't waste time snatching my arm, dragging me back through the chaos towards Silas, who stood by Talon. He had no idea just how bad things were until he stopped in his tracks, our eyes sweeping over our mother's lifeless body in Talon's arms.

"No—" he gasped, dropping his grip on me. "Mom..."

My father's eyes met ours as he tried to remain composed. "The blast hit her. She died instantly."

"What caused the explosion?" I finally asked, hoping for clarity. At my question Talon, Silas, and Pollux all looked at each other as if keeping a secret they didn't want me to know.

"It doesn't matter," Pollux snipped, "she's gone."

The care and concern he had just shown moments ago was gone, and with it, a void of hatred had replaced it. Whatever they were dealing with they didn't want me to know the details. And realizing that irritated me only further. My fists clenching and unclenching at my side as I tried to keep my cool.

Silas stepped forward, placing a hand on my brother's shoulder, catching his attention. "She's with your sister now. Don't let this become a loss. Fate deemed it her time to go, and you know she was ready to join the others."

The others. He was speaking of my father's Damian, James, and Hale. Damian had gone to be with Cassie years ago, and

James and Hale ventured only a few years after when another operation had gone wrong—gas-like poison ended up taking them both.

"I know," he snapped, his jaw stiff and teeth clenched. "It was what she wanted."

Shaking his head, Silas dropped his hand before. "It was, and now it is time for Tate to fulfill his destiny."

Destiny?

"What the fuck are you talking about?" I murmured with confusion, my eyes glancing between Silas and Pollux. "What destiny?"

Pollux was quiet, his eyes locked onto our mother's body as a heavy sigh escaped his lips. "Things aren't as great as they should be, Tate. We're slowly losing our reign and Pandora as well as Faeryn are in danger because of their powers. Trixie is taking Pandora as we speak back to the kingdom of Tver."

"What?!" I gasped, my eyes wide with shock. "Why the hell didn't you tell me?!"

His eyes locked with mine, brows narrowed as anger filled his gaze. "When the hell was I supposed to do that, Tate? You never take anything seriously, and I don't have time to hold your hand while you play mommy's favorite!"

"Enough," Silas' snapped, "we don't have time for this bull-shit. The Hallow is lost to us again, and Tate is our only hope in finding it."

Pollux scoffed, rolling his eyes as he ran his hand through his hair, pacing around the clearing.

"He isn't ready, Silas. He's just a kid."

"Go fuck yourself, Lux. You don't know me," I snapped at him, crossing my arms over my chest. I didn't have a clue what they were talking about, but I wasn't going to let my brother stand here talking shit about me when he didn't even really know me.

Especially with my father standing nearby with my mother's dead body in his arms.

"Enough of this," Silas snapped at us both. "Right now isn't the place."

It didn't matter that Silas was trying to get us on the right path. It was as if Pollux hadn't heard a word as he stopped in his tracks and spun to face me, irritation and anger in his eyes as he clenched his fists at his side.

"Oh, don't I? You have no idea what's been going on, and with Deidra dead because of Moira...the chance of us finding the Hallow is slim."

"Don't say that," Silas replied. "Tatum can find the Hallow. It's been deemed so."

Pollux rolled his eyes. His lack of confidence in me was getting on my nerves. I didn't know what this Hallow thing was, but if they believed I was meant to find it, then I would.

Over the years, Pollux had never really taken the time to get to know me. He always acted like I was nothing but a burden to him, and because of that, I did act out every now and again. Though, maybe had he taken the time to make things right with me and the rest of our siblings, then perhaps we would have respected him more.

Maybe, we would have made things right and followed him like we were supposed to.

After all, I was the only one who had stayed in the pack out of us all.

The rest got out as soon as they were old enough. Pollux had just been too hard to live with.

Silas turned to me, his jaw clenched and eyes closed as Pollux and I stared at each other with so much hatred. He attempted to step towards me, his shoulders rising and falling, only for Silas's arm to thrust out, stopping him.

"Don't touch me," he snapped, shrugging Silas off.

"Well then. Don't act fucking stupid," Silas's snapped back. "Now he says he is ready so he's ready."

A maniacal laugh escaped Pollux as he stared at me with amusement dancing within his eyes. A darkness that seemed to find joy in the idea of me taking on whatever task it was that they needed me to do.

"I hope you are, brother because in order for you to help at all, you have to die and hope that fate selects you."

CHAPTER ONE

Thirty Years Later

Salem, Massachusetts.

More than a city known for the fanatics who came in search of supernatural adventures, Salem was a place that held history and power within it. A place humans of all kinds flocked to regularly to find solace in something magical and enchanting. Not that I could complain about something like that, I had done the same thing.

The only difference between me and the fanatics...I wasn't exactly human.

Too many times I ventured out at night in order to sate my hunger, and just like always, I found my victim willingly. It wasn't like I had a choice. It wasn't who I was, but instead, what I was.

A predator.

A predator constantly hunting, seeking my next fill for desire, which coursed through the veins of any man who crossed my path.

Years of practice had led me to control my urges more than others like me, which also got me classified as tame. But even if I was more tame than others, I still had trouble controlling myself sometimes.

Though I made sure that I never killed them. I refused to be like my mother in that aspect.

Tonight was no different. I had left work with every intention of going home, but the urge to feed took over, and I was forced to give in. So under the slowly darkening sky, I had made my way towards the nearest night club in search of my next fix that gave me what I needed and made me feel a hell of a lot more powerful afterwards.

Pulling my keys from my pocket, I placed them in the lock of my front door and turned the knob. Lavender and patchouli from the incense burners invaded my senses, welcoming me home.

My home wasn't much, but after the shit I had been through over the past few years, it was mine.

Walking into my small but spacious one-bedroom apartment, I smiled, happy to finally be home after a long day. Work had been agonizing, and though I hadn't expected to feed tonight, the offer that presented itself was too good to pass up.

"You're getting sloppy," a cool, sweet voice said from the shadows of my living room. I wasn't unfamiliar with the voice, and as she turned on the lamp on the table next to her, the dim yellow light filled the space around us. My smile fell.

"Sloppy, Claire?" I chuckled, setting my keys and purse down on the table next to the front door. "Never. I just finished up work."

The soft, green eyes of my sister narrowed while a smirk settled on her perfectly red lips. "Is that right? So, who was the delicious emo-kid with multiple ear piercings you feasted on earlier?"

I shouldn't have been surprised she spied on me. My sister had a thing for watching me so she could run back to our mother and tell her everything I was doing that didn't fit with the "code" of how we were supposed to live. Rolling my eyes, I moved further into the living room.

"He is like...twenty-four. I'd hardly call him a kid. Plus, I didn't kill him like you would have. I left him slightly...coherent."

The jab caused her to purse her lips in annoyance as she crossed her legs, laying her hands delicately on her lap. "Yeah, in an alley with his dick out. Not very classy, Taylor."

"Perhaps, but in the end, we both got pleasure in some sort of way."

With a sneer on her lips, she stared at me with disgust. "Doesn't change the fact that you left him the way you did."

It wasn't entirely my fault the guy ended up that way.

"Oh, stop being such a prude. He enjoyed it...mostly," I replied, thinking about the cocky guy who claimed he could make me scream his name in four languages. In the end, it turned out he was the one who ended up screaming right before he passed out.

My sweet sister Claire, as my mother would call her, was the last person I had wanted to see this evening. Ever since we were kids, she had been a pain in my ass and did everything she could to point out my flaws to make herself look better.

Like kissing Mommy Dearest's ass on the regular.

Something I wouldn't do.

"This has to stop—"

"If you came to lecture me, I'm not in the mood for it," I stated coldly, "so why don't you tell me why you're here instead, and make it quick."

I wasn't a stranger to her random visits. Every year she liked to pop up and surprise me with her antagonizing remarks, delivering messages to me from my mother that I ignored, unless delivered in person. In fact, the last time she came round, I ended up with a bullet hole in my thigh.

A story for another day.

"The warm welcome you give is always joyous," she replied with sarcasm.

I ignored her melodrama and walked towards my room. Her heels echoed against my hardwood floor, letting me know she was following me. I wanted to protest, but it was pointless. Claire always did what Claire wanted to do. "Mother wants you to move back home. It isn't safe out here on your own, and I agree."

Home. That wasn't something I had thought about in quite some time. The dull, asphyxiating feeling of being back at my childhood home was more like a nightmare than a dream. "No, thanks."

"Taylor, this is serious," she snapped.

"So is my shower, Claire," I called back as I turned to jump in.

"Damn it, Taylor!" she exclaimed, snatching my arm as I tried to step into my beautifully-tiled shower I had spent a fortune installing. I wasn't typically one to be nostalgic, but when I designed this bathroom, I did it to replicate the hot stone baths of my home. It was the only place that I had ever felt solace when I lived with my mother, and the only part of my childhood I allowed to follow me. "The hunters are closing in, and the only way we remain safe is together."

Glancing at her grip on my arm, I narrowed my eyes in anger as my lip curled to show her my irritation. Sister or not, she knew I hated being manhandled. "Move your hand, now."

She hesitated for a split second until it sunk in what she had done. The rapid haste in which she moved would make one question whether or not my skin had burnt her. However, it was simply because she knew what happened to the last person who had touched me without my consent.

I'd picked him up by his throat and made him beg for mercy.

"I'm sorry. Just, please...come home." She finally sighed. "It would make everyone feel better if we knew that you were actually safe."

Desperation was in her eyes, and rolling mine, I decided to entertain her. "Fine...I'll think about it."

It wasn't a yes, but I would take it into consideration as long as it meant she would drop the subject and leave me alone. The only thing I wanted to do was enjoy my shower in peace without the irritation of my sister trying to convince me to go home.

"That's all I ask," she said, excited by the prospect of me agreeing to what my mother wanted. After all, it wasn't often I said I would consider it. "I'll go for now. Enjoy your shower."

Twenty minutes later and freshly dressed in leggings and a tank top, I walked out into the living room with a glass of red wine on my mind. When I turned the corner, my sister's face came into view.

"I thought you would have gone by now," I admitted, passing where she sat headed towards the kitchen.

"Wow, hoping to get rid of me? I said that I would go, for now."

"Well, that was the hope, Claire. Why are you still here?" I replied, irritated.

Grabbing a goblet from the nearest cupboard, I tried to ignore her presence. Perhaps if I was cold enough, she would finally get the hint. Then again, that was always wishful thinking.

"I need to make sure you come back with me. Mom's words, not mine."

Snapping my gaze to Claire, I pulled the cork from the already opened bottle and frowned. "I said I would consider it. I'm damn sure not going right now, and you can't stay here."

The pout that appeared on her lips grated on my last nerve. She tried to pout her way out of everything and it may have worked on my mother, but it wouldn't work on me. Giving her a pointed, indifferent glare, she crossed her arms over her chest. "Fine, but I'll be back in two weeks. I have to go take care of some stuff in New York anyways. Make sure you're ready."

Taken back by her comment, I glared at her. "If you have to go there, why the hell did you come here? This conversation could have been a phone call or better yet, a text."

Standing, she fixed her designer clothes as if she had to look perfect everywhere she went. If we didn't look similar, there was no way anyone would ever know we were related. She and I were complete opposites. "Two weeks, Taylor."

Two weeks, my ass...I wasn't going.

"Yep. Call first before you come back."

The sound of the front door closing was a blessing. I wasn't sure how she had gotten in since she didn't have a key, but I wouldn't be surprised if she hadn't charmed the building manager at some point.

Pouring my wine to the rim, I sipped it as I headed towards my lush gray sofa. The white, furry throw blanket called my name as I made myself comfortable and picked up the remote. Late night binge watching of my favorite shows was on the top of my to do list, and as I flipped on the TV, the news came on, causing me to frown.

First, she breaks into my place, and then she fucks with my TV.

I never watched the news, and the fact it was on meant my sister had purposely made sure to put it on this channel. In an attempt to ignore it, I went to hit the guide button, only to stop when they started talking about a string of murders in Salem.

Salem was the closest major town to where I lived—Marblehead—and my hunting grounds. I chose the opportunity to work in Salem while living outside so as to not draw attention to myself. The small book and alchemy shop I owned was a cute attraction for the tourists who flocked to Salem every year for its witchy atmosphere.

Their desire to obtain a special remedy for illnesses, or broken hearts, was endless.

It was also something I loved. I was gifted in making herbal remedies and the art of alchemy. My remedies have helped so many people since I had moved here—even if it was slightly tainted with real magic, something most of the tourists wished they had.

I had made a few friends here, but none of them knew what I was, and that's how I stayed safe. Stay mysterious and sweet and never let anyone in.

Was it lonely?

Sometimes.

I made do as I always did.

But being low key was how I had been able to stay hidden for so long. As the news anchor talked about the many men killed over the past year, I kept listening. They hadn't been able to connect the murders in the past, but after the latest one, they finally had clues to close in on the killer.

I wasn't sure what supernatural creature had done this, but it wasn't good. The last thing I wanted was this kind of attention being drawn to the area I fed. There was no way the mundane law enforcement would be able to find this creature. As much as I liked to stay to myself, it dawned on me I was going to have to help them in the long run.

I couldn't lose the only thing allowing me to stay in one place.

With a groan, I pulled out my phone and texted my sister. "It wasn't me."

It didn't take but a moment for her to reply, and her text made my brows knit together in confusion. "Are you sure? Keep watching."

"Keep watching? The hell is her problem—"

The last thing I expected was for a picture of the guy I had fed from tonight to pop up on the screen. Hewas labeled as the last murder victim of this pristine serial killer, and my heart sank. When I left him, he was alive. The fact he was dead shocked me.

"It wasn't me...he was alive when I left him," I replied with frustration, trying to understand how this happened. "Someone is framing me."

The bubbles showed my sister was typing a long message, which made me worry even more. She wasn't usually one with a lot to say unless she was in your face. Dealing with her in this kind of situation made things more complicated. She was playing the middleman between my mother and I, and this latest stunt would make it even easier for my mother to get me home.

"I'm not sure what to tell you, but Mother has seen this and we are both concerned. You're making a mess of things and getting sloppy. If this isn't a wake up call to come home, then you're more delusional than I thought."

Fuck...if I didn't figure out what the hell was going on—my future here was done.

CHAPTER TWO

Several days had passed after the police found that boy's dead body. My sister hadn't bothered reaching out to me again, and for the last few days, I had barely slept. My thoughts kept running straight back to that poor guy I had fed from. It wasn't possible. There was no way I had killed him. The only problem was...he was actually dead.

No matter how I tried to spin it.

The only thing I could think of was maybe someone else had found him after I had left him. I mean, it wasn't exactly good. I had just left him laying there, half exposed in the middle of a dark alley where any supernatural creature or human could find him, but I did.

Now because of that, I found myself watching everything more closely.

Every day since then, when I came to work, I'd find the police patrolling the streets, or someone would come in asking to put up a flyer so they could find any bit of information they could about the guy that had died recently. And every time they did, my heart raced with anticipation that someone was going to find out I had something to do with it.

I had to remind myself, though. I had been careful. I had covered my tracks and nobody had seen me...at least no one except my sister.

Fuck...what am I doing? If she saw me then God knows who else fucking did. So stupid!

Running my hand through my hair, I gazed out the front window of my shop again. People milled around dressed in everything from normal clothing to witchy, goth outfits, all preparing for the events coming up in the next few weeks.

The month of October, or more importantly, Halloween, was the busiest time of the year for Salem. It was when people from all over the world flocked here to take part in the town's festivities and possibly find their own spark of magic.

It was also the time of year I dreaded, being a succubus. It wasn't easy and during October, it made things a lot harder for me. The Harvest full moon was when my power was at its fullest, and no matter the control I had on myself, I would be driven by uncontrollable hunger on that night.

A night that drove fear into my damned soul every year.

"Excuse me," a snappy girl with bright pink hair and a nose piercing said, drawing my attention from the window. "Are you gonna stand there all day, or are you going to help me?"

I was all up for customer service and putting up with the "Karen" type of persona, or whatever it was these kids called it these days. But what I wasn't going to do was have her cause an issue in my store. "I'm sorry. I didn't realize that you needed help."

Scoffing, she rolled her eyes. "Are you blind then? We have been standing over by the candles for like fifteen minutes."

"Fifteen minutes?" I repeated, my lips turning into a grin. "That's interesting because I'm pretty sure you walked in the door five minutes ago."

Glancing over to the dark brunette in fishnets, a miniskirt and a rather revealing low cut top, she shifted from one foot to the other as if uncomfortable about the interaction between her friend and I.

"Are you calling me a liar?" The bright pink-haired girl snapped, "You literally have one job, and you can't do that right. Where's your manager?"

The laughter that left my throat at this girl's attitude caught me by surprise. Typically, I didn't have issues with people who shopped here. Yet there were always those few special times a year I would have young entitled girls come into my shop thinking they could act however they wanted because it was how they acted at home.

Leaning over the counter, I rested my elbows upon the wood and smiled at her. "Oh sweetheart, that attitude may have worked where you came from, but it won't work here."

"Excuse me? Who the fuck—"

"Alright, I'm going to stop you right there...you aren't going to act like that in my store. So I don't know what you and your friend needed, but you can go ahead and take your ass on out of here before you regret what ends up happening next."

The bell chimed above my door, where a tall, handsome piece of ass with short brown hair and deep blue eyes walked in and glanced around, clearly looking for something. Something that I was more than happy to help him with.

The girl seemed to have noticed the man as well and quickly swept her hair back from her face as she fixed her top, pushing her breasts up, seemingly having forgotten she was having words with me.

"Don't bother looking to buy anything in here," she said to him, her voice laced with an irritating seductiveness that made me internally cringe. "This woman is a bitch and doesn't care about her customers."

For the first time, he turned to her, almost as if he hadn't even noticed she was standing there and smiled. "Oh, is that right? I was hoping to get help with something."

"Oh, I'd be happy to help you," she said, perking up at his comment. "I'd be way more helpful than this peasant."

Peasant? Was she being fucking serious right now?

Again, I laughed. This woman was absolutely delusional. At my laughter, he turned to look at me with a sexy grin that completely caught me off guard. "I appreciate your offer, but I think I'll take my chances with the woman behind the counter."

"Seriously?" she sneered, casting her gaze to me, "but she's a bitch."

"Yeah, maybe she is," he replied. "But I heard how you were acting when I came in, and it was less than impressive. So why don't you and your friend go ahead and leave before things get really awkward."

The pink-haired girl and her friend stared at the man in shock before she huffed, stopping her foot as she stormed towards the front door, her friend hot on her heels. I couldn't contain the laughter that left me the moment they exited my store, the chime once again echoing as I shook my head in amusement.

"Do you often get people in here like that?"

Looking towards the man, I paused to admire his chiseled jaw and well-cut physique before letting a small grin slide across my lips. "No, but today must have been a special kind of day."

"Special indeed." He chuckled, his eyes casting a quick glance over his shoulder to where the girls had disappeared before looking back at me.

Staring at him, I waited for him to ask whatever it was he needed, but when nothing but awkward silence fell between us, I decided to break the ice. "So...what can I help you with?"

"Oh, well, I was actually going door to door asking people if they had seen anything out of the ordinary around here," he said as he took a step closer towards the counter. There was something about the way his aura shimmered with a cerulean hue that intrigued me. Even the slight hint of an accent lingered on the few words he had said, made me curious as to where he had come from. I was accustomed to speaking to people from all over the world, but something about him...seemed otherworldly. I couldn't put my finger on it.

"That's an odd thing to be going around asking people. Why would you want to know if there is anything weird going on?"

"You don't watch the news," he deadpanned. *Shit. He's talking about the murders, and its pretty fucking obvious he isn't from around here.*

"Oh, that. I don't often have time to watch the news."

"I haven't had someone tell me that one yet." He didn't seem overly bothered by what had happened, instead he just seemed interested in me, or maybe that was me just being presumptuous.

"Not unless I have to. I prefer to live carefree instead of worrying, like the rest of these people around here. I mean, one little bit of juicy gossip in these parts and everyone is in an uproar."

He laughed as he nodded his head in understanding. "I get it."

Something about him seemed different from most of the men I have met traveling into Salem. It was as if someone had picked him up out of a movie set and dropped him into my shop.

"So since I can't help you with what you came in here for...is there something else I can help you with?" I asked after a moment of silence passed between us. His eyes searched mine before he broke eye contact, letting them drift around the shop.

"This place is nice...you set it up yourself?"

Weird subject change since he came in here asking about the murders, but okay?

"Um, yep," I replied, popping the 'p', "why, are you interested in this kind of stuff?"

A snort of amusement escaped him as he shook his head, his eyes finding mine once more. "Not me, but someone very close to me is...into this kind of stuff."

"Well, take a look around and see if you can find her something nice."

He hesitated for a moment as a smile spread across his face. "Who said it was a she?"

It was my turn to laugh as a smile crossed my lips. He wasn't serious, was he? It was obvious he had someone waiting for him back home. "Come on now…a guy like you? You're definitely taken by someone."

He didn't bother denying the statement, nodding his head and slowly turned towards the door to my shop. It wasn't the first time a man had come in here before acting flirtatious when he knew he wasn't available. Shit like that… I didn't let bother me though, it was what it was.

After he was gone, I stood in silence, pondering over everything. The shit happening in our city wasn't normal, and trust me, I knew what was normal and what wasn't. I wasn't fucking normal—in fact; I was far from it.

Though, this was the first time the things going on were hitting a little too close to home.

If I was going to feed again, I was really going to have to be more careful.

CHAPTER THREE

<u>Tatum</u>

Something about this town didn't sit well with me. The air chilled me to the bone and the power that resonated under its surface seemed to taunt me with unusual expectations. I wasn't quite sure why it took so long for the organization to come to Salem, but now that we were here, my task was proving to be far more difficult.

Fifteen years I had searched for a solution to our problems in this realm. Every lead that came in and every mission that happened, I was there. Ready at the forefront, praying that the key I needed would show itself so I could leave this god awful place. However, it was all simple wishful thinking on my part.

Instead, I was stuck here, still wandering.

Waiting for what I needed with company I didn't care for.

"Hey Tate, did you get any info?" Derrick—my supposed partner—called from outside the shop front two doors down.

He was a lazy son-of-a-bitch most of the time, but since we arrived in Salem less than twenty-four hours ago, he seemed to be overly excited at doing his job.

"No, same shit, different store," I replied, looking over my shoulder through the window at the fiery woman with violet hair and bright azure colored eyes.

She was different from the other women around here. Something about her screamed, carefree but mysterious. Not to mention I had this feeling as if I'd known her for a long time. It was comforting, even if we had never met before.

"What's wrong with you?" Derrick laughed as I glanced back at him. His gaze was now locked on the woman I had been staring at.

"Nothing, just thinking about something."

"You mean that hot piece of ass?" he replied, a look on his face way more suggestive than it needed to be.

"Do you really have to speak about women like that?"

This wasn't the first time he had made comments about women that made me cringe. He was a piece of work and went through women like he changed his underwear. The urge to throttle him every time he made grotesque comments grew stronger and stronger.

It wasn't that I was a prude. It was just annoying as hell listening to him.

"I don't know." He chuckled. "Do you really have to be constantly oblivious to gorgeous women every time we go somewhere? I mean...come on, man. You have to have fun sometimes."

Fun. A word I would often use when it came to my line of work. Sure, when I finally was able to go home, I would try to take some initiative to settle down, but right now, that wasn't the case. I was on a job, and I needed to stay focused. Unlike my partner, who seemed to think with his dick more than the head on his shoulders.

A disgruntled scoff left my lips as I moved past him, headed in the direction he had come from. I had been in Salem for less than twenty-four hours, and it already felt like a waste of my time. Although Silas said this was where Finnick had said I could possibly find her.

And all of my research had only further confirmed their claims.

Though, the feeling I was being misled played heavily in the back of my mind.

"Tate, come on man...let's go get some food. There is no way we are going to find anything right now. We need to regroup...preferably at the nearest diner."

Again with his annoying antics. If it wasn't him trying to get laid, it was him trying to fill his stomach. Stopping in my tracks, I let out a heavy breath and cast him a glance over my shoulder with an irritated expression. "If you want to turn in for the night and get food, then go. I have a few more things I want to check out, and then I'll meet you back at the hotel."

It was against protocol to split up. Derrick's brows rose slightly as his eyes widened. He stared at me for a moment, but instead of arguing, he nodded. "Okay, but don't do stupid shit, Tate. We don't know this place well enough to be going solo. If you find something...call me."

Call him? The internal laughter coursing through me forced a smirk to fall across my lips. "Sure."

Derrick had worked with me long enough to know I wasn't going to listen to anything he had to say. Yet, he still felt the need to give me advice. When he realized I was done with the conversation, he turned and hurried away.

The day was still young, and though part of me wondered what it would bring, I knew I had to get a better grasp at what I was dealing with in this place, not to mention the people. I let my eyes drift once more to the sign hanging above the shopkeeper's door. The woman's eyes floated through my mind, a connection I couldn't forget.

It made little sense why she stuck out in my mind so much after such a short greeting, but in a city like Salem, she was the only face that remained clear. Which made me wonder if I was missing something.

I tried to keep myself focused on the task at hand. A task that didn't involve Derrick or the monster we were supposed to be hunting. My priorities were elsewhere tonight and had been for the past decade. Though the only way I had gotten close to finding what I needed was because I had joined the cult-like organization—Elite Humanity—and made my way to the top.

Not that I would stay there long. Once I got what I needed, I was out of this shit hole.

Taylor

The sky darkened outside my shop, so I was quick to close up. I made my way across the wooden floors, going from window to window, drawing curtains and turning off the glowing neon lights that welcomed people after dark. My shop, a place that wouldn't hold late night visitors today.

Uneasiness had settled into my bones since this morning, and the more I stayed away from the security of my home, the more the need to run increased.

Run...that wasn't something I had done in a long time. Today it felt oddly right.

With everything transpiring in the city lately, I found myself overwhelmed. Not to mention my wandering mind kept going to the man who had entered my shop earlier. God, it had been so long since a delicious, well-sculpted man had set foot into my place. And though the monster inside me cried to take pleasure in him...I couldn't.

It was too risky to feed with the city on high-alert.

Glancing around my now darkened shop, I smiled. From the creaking wooden floors to the dust that had settled upon shelves and counters—I loved it here. However, the past few days it didn't bring me the same safety I had once felt before. The idea of having to leave because of the murders wasn't something I wanted to contemplate, but if hunters really were coming to town, it was something I would have to take into serious consideration.

I didn't want to end up back at my mother's and though I had managed to survive this far on my own without protection, I had to be careful.

Closing the door behind me, I stepped out onto the cobbled path outside. My eyes instinctively closed as I inhaled fresh air and basked beneath the moonlight. As a creature of night, these were moments I loved the most; the comfort of the moon and the warmth of the darkness that always wrapped around me.

But again, it didn't sate me tonight as usual. Instead, a cold hand seemed to grasp at my soul, telling me to leave. Telling me to go far away before it was too late.

Locking the door, I made my way down the path. Many of the shops stayed open, and as I peeked into a few as I passed, smiling customers laughed inside. It was the same as it always was, minus the rude few customers who graced us with their presence every once and a while. People were happy, and simply excited to be in a mystical place like Salem.

Turning the corner, I made my way down the alley and headed for the parking lot. I had traveled this path so many times, but as I stepped into its darkened shadows, the atmosphere felt off. The hair on the back of my neck rose.

I wasn't alone.

"Hey there, little lady," a deep voice called out, laced with malice.

Ahead of me, half-way from the exit, was the darkened silhouette of a man. The last thing I expected to deal with was some asshole who wanted to ruin my night, but the next two steps I took towards him made me realize he was anything but a man.

In fact, he wasn't even human.

Fucking great.

"I'm not interested in whatever words you have to give me, shifter," I called out, making it aware I knew what he was and making it known I wasn't human either. Though this breed of shifter tended not to be as understanding as others. Fucking bear shifter.

The golden-orange iris of his eyes shined through the darkness, causing me to cringe at what was to come next. "You have a smart mouth on you, girl. I'm going to enjoy playing with you."

"Oh God, you're being serious, aren't you?" I replied, disgustedly, "this isn't going to go the way you want."

Laughter again escaped him. "Oh, but I think it is. You're just too damn beautiful to pass up."

Swiftly, he lunged at me, racing down the alleyway. No doubt to attack me. The problem was I wasn't in the mood, nor did I have the patience to deal with this shifter. I was tired and starving.

When he got close to me, the secret power that built inside me loosened. Hand outstretched, I grabbed the shifter by his throat and slammed him against the brick alley wall. My eyes were undoubtedly glowing the fierce azure color when I tapped into my power. I didn't feed off supernatural creatures because of the principle behind it, but right now, this particular supernatural had simply pissed me off.

"YOU BITCH!" he growled as he thrashed out at me. The power radiating off me was enough to keep him pinned, so I didn't get hurt, but I wouldn't last long. It never did.

"Are you the one killing all the people around here?"

A sneer appeared across his face as he growled at me again. "Let me go, and you'll find out."

"You know you're making this harder than it needs to be. You shouldn't even be in these parts, shifter. The city is off limits to your kind of violence."

"Says the witch who wields magic!" Thrashing again, my magic slowly slipped as I tried to keep him in place. However, the fact that he called me a witch struck a nerve. I wasn't a fucking witch, and him assuming was an insult. It wasn't that I had anything against them, hell, my mentor had been one.

But it was like calling a wiccan a wolf, or calling a wolf a bear...it was absurd.

"First off...you're incredibly rude," I snapped, narrowing my eyes, the hunger inside me coming alive as I stepped closer. "Second...I'm no fucking witch."

Most people thought that succubi only fed through sexual pleasure, and perhaps that was right in some cases. But not entirely. There were things we chose to let the mortal world believe to keep our secrets. Leaning close to him, my magic jolted his head back, causing his mouth to open.

A ravenous desire to punish him grew stronger and stronger as my magic seemed to call to him, draining him slowly of the life force he clung to. The light in his eyes grew dim with each passing second, until the sound of a throat clearing behind me caused me to lose my focus.

The shifter quickly dropped to the floor, still alive but un-conscious.

"Shit," I mumbled under my breath, preparing to turn around. I had gotten caught, which has never happened. Now, I was going to have to think through this quickly. The only problem was, as I slowly turned around, I came face-to-face with the man from my shop.

His cool demeanor caught me off guard as he stood there, twenty feet from where I was. A raised brow and a smirk decorated his face as he slightly tilted his head to the side, his arms crossed over his chest as if he was observing me. I wasn't sure if it was a good thing or a bad thing.

Most of all, I didn't understand why he seemed so calm.

"I must admit...I wasn't expecting it to be you."

Wait, what the fuck?

"Uh, I don't know what you think you saw, but I can explain," I replied as I tried to come up with a logical explanation.

His smile only grew at my words as he leaned against the brick wall, his eyes trailing down to the creature behind me. "Really? I'd love to hear..."

"Uh, it's part of a Salem Halloween thing we're doing. He and I were just acting."

"Acting..." he chuckled.

"Yep." I glanced back at the man on the ground. "This is Ted. He takes his acting seriously. Can't break character, ain't that right, Ted."

He pushed off from the wall, his smile falling as he shook his head from side to side. "Do you really think anyone would buy that explanation?"

Shit. Of course they wouldn't. I fucking suck at lying.

"I'm not lying."

"Yes, you are," He replied. "The shifter attacked you, didn't he?"

Shifter...how the fuck would he know...oh my god.

"What are you talking about...what's a shifter?"

Rolling his eyes, he frowned. "Stop lying. You're really terrible at it. I know what you are."

Before I could say anything, a silver pendant on a chain around his neck caught my eyes. The light from a nearby street lamp caused a glint to appear within the shadows.

That crest...I know that crest. Why do I know that crest?

It took a moment for things to click in my mind. The fast realization of where I had seen it before caused my heart to all but burst as panic quickly set in. "No fucking way...you're—"

"A hunter...yeah, I can explain that."

Chapter Four

The last thing I expected was to end up in an alley with an unconscious shifter behind me, and the man I had ogled over in my shop in front of me. It seemed like my nice and peaceful life had taken a chaotic twist. Maybe most people would have just ran with it, but I couldn't help but be annoyed.

He was a hunter. My sister tried to warn me they would end up coming here and the exact reason why she said I needed to go home. But of course, I didn't fucking listen.

As usual.

"Look," I replied, holding my hand up as my eyes darted between the man in front of me to the unconscious shifter behind me. "It isn't what it looks like..."

"Is that right?" He looked down at the man. "So you didn't just try to drain him of his life, Succubus?"

Shit...shit shit shit. God, I'm a fucking idiot.

My heart was beating out of my chest and I probably looked panicked to this man, but that's because I was. Hunters were killers. They never bothered to know the truth about anything. All they did was kill creatures who were inno-cent...well, mostly innocent.

"I'm just leaving...he attacked me...I—" I replied, stumbling over myself like a naïve school girl.

The man took a step forward, so I took one to the side. If I was careful enough, I'd be able to get a clear shot down the alley and beeline straight towards my car. However, if I wasn't careful, this man could kill me and though I do feed from humans, I wasn't a killer.

At least, not in the last few years.

"Look, I think you and I should talk." The man was trying to reason with me and there was no way I was going to let that happen. I was already fucked because he knew who I was, where I worked, and if I wasn't careful, he would probably figure out where I lived.

"I'm sorry, but I really have to go." I spun on my heels and bolted as fast as I could down the alleyway. My feet hit the concrete with desperate force as I ran towards my car. The only problem was I wasn't as fast as I thought, and a firm arm around my waist caught me mid-stride, stopping me in my tracks.

"Let me go!" I screamed, struggling against the man who spun me, pinning me against the side of a nearby black SUV.

"Will you just stop, for fuck's sake, lady? I'm not going to hurt you."

"Bullshit!" I replied angrily as I continued to struggle. "You're all the same. You're all killers."

An annoyed sound came from the man as he spun me around in his arms, so I was forced to look up into his eyes. "Do I look like a killer to you? I'm trying to help you."

What...?

"Is this a joke? Do you get off on scaring young women and then tricking them into trusting you right before you fucking kill them?!" I snapped, brows narrowed as I stared into his gorgeous eyes. He was incredibly handsome.

He carried himself as if he had all the confidence in the world and made me bite at my bottom lip as I tried to contain my excitement. Not to mention those beautiful deep eyes; I wanted to stare at him and forget about all the shit I was going through. I couldn't think like this though. No matter how tempting he was, I was in the arms of a hunter.

"It's no joke. I'm trying to help you, but if you don't stop, you're going to get yourself killed."

A look of determination in his eyes made me question my sanity. I stopped fighting him and my body seemed to relax. Something about this man made me feel uneasy, but at the same time, I was completely intrigued.

"Why would you want to help me? You're a hunter." I was taking a shot at trying to figure him out, and as a look of amusement crossed his eyes, I felt incredibly uncertain of my current situation.

"Well, I'd be happy—"

The sound of squealing tires on asphalt drew our attention as a black car came flying around the corner into the parking lot. It stopped only a short distance from us. The door opened and another man appeared, looking nothing like the man in front of me.

He was shorter than my mystery man, with reddish brown curly hair, and a clean face with greedy green eyes. He—most likely another hunter—was definitely more cocky about his position and the moment his eyes landed on the two of us, a wicked smile spread across his face.

"I got a tip about a problem in the area...is everything alright?" The man glanced between me and the mystery man in front of me, who still had me caged. I had no doubts now this newcomer was a hunter. His entire demeanor screamed dominance and part of me wondered if this was how I was going to die.

"Yeah, Derrick. The subject is in the alley. It attacked this woman when she was walking to her car, but I managed to get him unconscious for the time being."

What the fuck? Did he just lie for me?!

Eyes wide, I stared at the man in front of me with curiosity. He lied to this other guy for me, and I didn't understand why. The man didn't even fucking know me.

"Okay," the man said slowly. "Well, get her out of here, Tate. We have shit to take care of."

Tate. Was that short for something else?

Tate nodded slowly to the man, who quickly disappeared down the dark alleyway to take care of the shifter I had left. Part of me felt bad that the shifter was going to more than likely be killed, but I didn't take pity on anyone who would purposely try to attack an innocent woman for no reason.

Not that I'm innocent, but it was the principle of it.

"You need to get out of here now," Tate whispered into my ear, causing the hairs on the back of my neck to stand. I closed my eyes, letting his deep, sultry voice wrap around me. "We need to talk...tonight, preferably."

Talk? What the hell...

"Why?" I asked, pulling away as I stared at him in confusion. My mind swirled over why he would want to speak with me considering he was a hunter and should instead be trying to kill me.

My eyes trailed over his face, searching for the answers I wanted, but also searching for any sign of him possibly messing with my head. Tate stood there though, eyes set on me with a rigid jaw, no longer trying to hold me back from running. His eyes glanced back towards the alley before landing back on me.

"Because...it's to save your life. Now, go."

Turning, he walked away, leaving me standing near the black SUV bewildered as I tried to understand what the fuck had just happened.

"I need a drink," I gasped as I turned and made my way towards my car that sat on the other side of the lot.

There was no way in hell I was going to wait around any longer than I had to when Tate and the other Hunter were present. The moment I got into my vehicle and the engine roared to life, I departed, heading out of Salem towards my home without question.

I wasn't sure why the hunter had spared me, and I don't think I will ever understand.

But I wasn't going to miss the opportunity for my life to be spared.

As the roads and trees passed by as I drove, I couldn't help but feel relieved. I was alive for another day. Or at least for right now. And as much as I didn't want to admit it, my home was no longer safe. I had to get out.

Time seemed to go by slowly as I made my way from Salem back to my small town. My apartment building came into view ahead of me. The blacked windows of many apartments sitting tall against the aged red and white bricked building towered over me as I turned into the blacktop parking lot.

Usually, when I came home, it was with the excitement of relaxing or perhaps getting ready to go out, but that wasn't the case. My anxiety was through the roof, and more than anything, I wanted to get out of here as soon as I could. I didn't care if Tate said he was trying to help me. Shit, for all I knew, it was some sick mind game he was playing with me.

The only thing I could distinguish out of all my emotions was fear.

Fear for the unknown. Fear of dying. But most of all, the fear of having to admit my mother was right. I didn't belong in the world I was in, and I didn't have anyone outside of my family to turn to. At least, not in the supernatural world. I kept myself separated from society for so long, I didn't know anyone anymore. At least not since Deidra and especially not around Salem.

Stepping out of my car, I slammed the door behind me and bolted towards the main door. I couldn't get inside fast enough. When my feet hit the steps, I took them two at a time.

As my door came into view, my keys fumbled in my hands, out of breath and more than flustered. I'm sure to anyone else I would have looked like I was running from a killer—which, I mean, I was—but in reality; I had already outwitted them and gotten to safety.

"What the fuck..." I muttered as I entered my apartment, slamming my back against the door and shutting it as I tried to catch my breath.

"You know you're a lot faster than you look."

My breath caught in my throat as my eyes flew open. The dark, sultry voice that had saved me not so long ago made fear flow through me once more. There, in front of me in the middle of my living room, standing within the shadows, was the same figure I had seen not long ago.

Tate.

There was no fucking way he knew where I lived! Shit, there was no way he got here before me! I had seen him as I left that parking lot. He had entered the alley behind that other guy.

How did he end up in my living room?

"What the fuck?" I gasped.

"I told you...we need to talk."

CHAPTER FIVE

"What the fuck?"

Tate approached me from the shadows as the words passed my lips. A cool smirk played across his plump pink lips. Broad shoulders and a firm build would usually make me swoon, but right now, I was on guard.

"Look, I know you're probably confused, but I promise I can explain." He pulled his hands from his pockets, holding them up as if to say he meant no harm.

I instinctively tried to avoid him, quickly dashing towards my kitchen. I went for the butcher knife, tucked safely away in a draw, only to be stopped in my tracks. Again, another firm grasp around my waist pulled me back, smashing me into a firm chest. "Don't do that. I saved you, remember?"

"You're a fucking hunter!" I screamed, only to have his hand come down over my mouth.

"Please don't do that. You don't want your neighbors hearing, do you?" He wasn't wrong. These walls were paper thin, and having unwanted attention wouldn't be a good thing.

"Now, if I let you go, will you please just let me explain what I'm doing here?"

As much as I wanted to say no and kill him before making a break for it, something inside me was curious to know why he let me go before. Why would a hunter help me after everything he saw? None of it made sense, and that worried me.

Nodding my head, I stilled as he cautiously released his hold on me. I could have made my move again, but I didn't. Instead, I turned around to face him. His massive frame towered over me. I was scared because something about him made me feel...wanting.

"You need to stop manhandling me."

It was the first thing I could think of to say. When it slipped from my mouth, I instantly regretted it. His brows shot up, a cool smile in place with amusement in his eyes.

"Oh, yeah?" He chuckled. "Perhaps don't go for the knives, and I won't have to manhandle you...even though I can tell you actually enjoy it."

My mouth dropped open. He was right, but I would never fucking admit that to him. "So sure of yourself, aren't you?"

"Maybe," he replied, shrugging his shoulders. "Now, can we talk?"

My eyes connected with his as I tried to search for some lie to what he was saying. I contemplated the situation. It was clear he wasn't going to leave until he talked about something. So, against my better judgment, I gave in.

"We can talk in the living room," I muttered as I turned back towards the cabinet behind me before going to the fridge.

"You're not going for more weapons, are you?"

"No," I replied through gritted teeth.

"Okay...well, aren't you going to join me?"

I reached into my fridge to pull out a bottle of wine. "If I'm going to deal with this right now after the night I had, then I need a drink."

The cold look I gave him was all he needed to know how serious I was. Nodding, he turned and made his way into the living room, sitting in my favorite chair. Something that annoyed me considering it was white, and he could have gotten it dirty doing things hunters do—like kill people.

"If you get my chair dirty, I will kill you."

His eyes locked onto me as I made my way towards the sofa and sat adjacent to him. I didn't care if he was here to talk or not. I wasn't going to take any chances with this man. My mind was wracking over the various areas in my home where other weapons had been stored.

The knife behind my television. The baseball bat by my bedroom door.

The gun in my nightstand.

Something my mother hadn't liked, but right now, I was thankful I got it.

"You don't have to be afraid of me. I won't hurt you."

"Says the hunter sitting in my living room," I replied, raising a brow as I watched him silently laugh to himself.

"Ah–yes. Well, I wouldn't exactly call myself a *hunter*, per se."

Was he being serious?

"Is that right?" I asked, "then what would you call yourself? A fairy godmother? I mean, shit, you're a hunter named Tate who saved a succubus you don't know, and then committed a crime by breaking into my house to have a *chat.*"

He blinked, my sarcasm thick in the air. I half expected him to snap at me. Maybe change his mind about killing me. But instead, he stared at me. The heat of his gaze caused my stomach to flutter as I tried not to show how much his look affected me.

"I guess you could call it something like that," he finally replied as he cleared his throat, placing his foot on his knee. "Just because I was with a hunter doesn't mean that I am one. And by the way, my name is Tatum. My nickname is Tate."

Tatum. That name does sound better than Tate.

I didn't know what he was getting at or why he was here, but his comment only fueled my curiosity.

"That doesn't really make sense, but...I'll *hear* you out." I sighed, "even if it's against my better judgment."

His sound of amusement crossed my skin, causing the hairs on my arms to stand. My body seemingly acted on its own accord as I took a deep breath, my hand rubbing over my arm as I tried desperately to get myself together.

"My story is long, and we don't have time for that right now. However, what I can tell you is that you have a right to want to flee. In fact, you need to. It won't take long for the hunter organization to find you, especially after what happened today."

His words were like a glass of cold water over my skin. I knew it, but I also knew he wasn't done telling me everything. My mind raced with everything I needed to do, and where the hell I was going to go.

"Taylor..." It took me a moment to realize he said my name, though I didn't know how he knew it. His brows knitted together as I took another sip of my wine and smiled.

"Sorry, continue."

He nodded with a seriousness in his eyes. "Very well. As I was saying, you have a day or two before you need to worry. I cleaned up your trail, but it won't take long for them to catch on—"

"Why are you helping me, Tatum? Better yet, how the fuck do you even know this shit? You don't even know me!" I snapped, the anxiety of what was happening building inside me to the point I felt like I was going to explode. I had been careful for so long and in one night, my entire world was crumbling around me.

He was quiet as he seemed to think over his answer. Blue eyes stared at me with curiosity as he clasped his hands in front of him, bringing them to rest against his lips. The same lips I couldn't stop staring at no matter how much I wanted to.

"Because I need your help with something."

There it was. He wasn't doing this because he was a nice guy. He was doing this because he needed something. Something I would have to give him for my freedom.

This wasn't the first time a man, or another supernatural, had brought this kind of deal to me. I had met too many bad people over the years who loved getting their hands on creatures like me. Rare supernaturals with the ability to seduce and kill their prey with ease. All because they saw us as easy and manipulating women who could do their dirty work.

"I'm not killing anyone. That isn't who I am."

"I'm not asking you to." There was sincerity behind his words that I didn't miss. Perhaps I was completely misreading the situation. Then again, this was what he wanted—to get me comfortable, so I let my guard down.

So many conflicting thoughts swirled through my mind, and I tried on more than one occasion to get rid of them, to give him the benefit of the doubt, but I couldn't. I didn't know this man, and I wasn't one to trust easily. That was how I had gotten hurt before.

"Okay…so make this easy, and tell me what it is you want."

The moment was taking too long. I wasn't sure if he was simply stalling or having a hard time explaining what he wanted. His mouth opened and closed before a smile graced his lips again, and with it, words finally escaped him.

"What do you know of Elder Hallow?" His question froze me from the inside out. No one should have known about Elder Hallow. It had been a well-guarded secret for so long, and to hear him—it shook me deeply to know a man who was associated with hunters knew about it.

Elder Hallow wasn't just a place, but a magical aspect of the supernatural world that had been hidden for centuries. Without it, the balance fell into chaos. I had to throw him off the trail.

"I don't know what you're talking about," I replied clearly.

"I think you do know."

Determination set in his gaze, telling me he wasn't going to let this go. I didn't care what he wanted; the Hallow wasn't something I would ever give up. "If you're not going to kill me, I think it's time that you leave."

Standing, I made my way back towards the kitchen. The moment Tatum left, I was gone from this place. As much as I didn't want to listen to what my mother and sister had told me, I couldn't deny they were right. Whatever was going on in this place was drawing too much attention, particularly to me.

And that was something I didn't want.

"Taylor, I can't go until I talk with you about this. I know you know what I'm speaking of. Elder Hallow is crucial to a situation I need to handle, and without it things could get really bad—"

Spinning around, I narrowed my eyes at him. "Look, I don't know what you're talking about. You have me mixed up with someone else, and the sooner you realize that I can't tell you anything, the better. Now, please go."

Tatum stood there, towering over me as he had since the moment I met him. His eyes broody, and the fun-loving demeanor he had before, gone. "If that's what you want. However, if you find yourself changing your mind about what I was going to ask of you, call me."

Reaching into his pocket, he pulled out a business card and handed it to me. The white piece of paper stretched out in his hand as I slowly reached out to take it. "A business card?"

He didn't bother answering me as a scoff left him. He turned and made his way towards my front door, the sound of it opening and closing caused my eyes to drift from the card in my hand to the space he had once occupied.

Everything that happened since I met him in my shop, to the event in the alley, to him showing up in my house was complete bullshit. Especially since the only thing he wanted to know about was my lineage.

My family had safely guarded the Elder Hallow for as long as I could remember. For a hunter to have this knowledge was unsettling. Something about Tatum in general was unsettling, and I couldn't help but wonder if everything that happened today had been staged.

Placing the card upon the counter, I pulled out my phone from my pocket and scrolled through to my sister's number. My thumb hesitated over the call button as I considered calling her to tell her what had happened. I was always the confident one, the only succubus in my family who didn't fall into the hierarchy bullshit my mother loved to pull.

Yet, even though I knew I should do the right thing and warn them, I couldn't. If I told them what happened, it would only make things more complicated for me. I'd never escape my mother's wrath, and I would be forever stuck in the hellhole she created. If I ran though...I'd be able to disappear. Right?

"Fuck it, I'm getting out of here," I said, turning my phone off as I slid it back into my pocket. If there were people coming for me, I wasn't about to stay here to wait for them.

CHAPTER SIX

<u>**Tatum**</u>

Once upon a time, I was someone who acted first before thinking through things. However, I worked years to grow out of my boyish notions to be the man my family needed me to be. Now that I had the chance to fix everything, I fell back into old ways and completely fucked it up.

Running my hand over my face, I groaned with irritation as I tried to find the clarity I needed to make my next move.

Taylor was wary of me, as she should be, but that didn't stop me from hoping she would try to understand me. With my associations with the hunters, I couldn't blame her. I would have been wary too.

The concrete outside her apartment building was damp with water from a light drizzle that had blessed the area. My mind raced as I fisted my hair, staring out into the darkened sky, wondering what I was going to do now. It had taken me years to find her, and now that I had, it was like I couldn't get it right.

As if my words refused to come out properly.

Her mesmerizing eyes wracked through my brain like a movie on repeat. The image of how she stared at me, her pouty lips, and the way she furrowed her brows when she was confused—all of it was more than I thought it would be.

I was here for a job. A task that had taken me years to even come close to accomplishing.

And now, I felt farther away from completing it than I was the day I started.

"Fuck!" My voice echoed against the night. I turned, making my way down the street. I hadn't driven here. No...I had used other gifts to make it to her apartment.

The problem now was trying to keep the hunters off her trail while I sorted out how to get her to cooperate. Little vixen was trying me, and where most would be pissed off, I was slightly turned on.

The shifter had been all too happy to mumble succubus while he had shifted in and out of consciousness. Those words alone had perked Derrick's attention and saved the shifter's life.

My phone rang from my pocket, and I stopped, a heavy breath escaping me. I knew who was calling, and it wasn't Derrick. It was far worse than that.

Pollux was waiting for my call and had been for a while. With every second I waited to give him news, things back home only got worse.

I hesitated before I answered it.

"Hello?"

"Did you find it?" he asked, gruff tone giving away his exhausted state. It had been years since our family had been whole. Years since things back home slowly fell apart, and I wished every moment to be as it once was.

I knew that wasn't possible.

"'It' would be a strong word to call 'her', but yes…I did."

"Her?" The shock in his wavering voice made me realize how much this meant to him. He had lost everything over the last few years and was keeping our home together by a thread as he waited to join the rest of us. My nephew was more than ready to take his place, but Pollux was unwilling to so easily give in. "No, the girl had the item that contained it. She isn't the item."

"No, Lux. It is her." I sighed. I wasn't sure we would find the trail to the Hallow here, but I should have known. After all, this place is where it all began. "I saw the power in her aura, Pollux. She is the fucking Hallow."

Laughter echoed through the phone at my words before he sighed again. "All those years of reading the scrolls and learning the history of our family, and you really did find what we were looking for."

"It wasn't really years, brother. You know very well that time is a funny thing to play with in our kind of situation."

Our family was anything but normal, and time here in the mortal realm constantly moved. Where I resided, it seemed to forever stand still, as if waiting for something we weren't ready to comprehend.

"Well, when are you bringing her back? We need to get this sorted soon."

There it was, the question I was waiting for him to ask. As much as I wanted to tell my brother I was on my way right then and there, I couldn't. One, she wasn't ready to trust me, let alone jump in a car or anything else to go visit my family, and two, I didn't know if the time was right.

"Well..." I paused, trying to find the words I needed to explain what had happened. "We have a problem with that."

Looking out across the darkened streets of her small town, I waited for his disappointment to rain down on me. "Tate, you know how important this is. We can't afford to have problems."

"I understand that, but I don't think she fully knows what she is yet. "

"What?" he gasped. "There is no way I believe that."

I pinched the bridge of my nose. "Yeah, that's what I thought, but you didn't see the look in her eyes tonight. She was terrified, and there was no way she could sense my true form. Had she and she wouldn't have acted in fear the way she did, Lux. The only fear from her was that of me being a *hunter*."

"Hunter...Tate, are you still messing with those people?"

Elite Humanity was the only way I was able to get an inside picture on everything going on. It was the only way to truly know where the attacks were happening, not to mention it allowed me to save as many supernaturals as I possibly could while hunting for the one I needed.

"They led me to her, Lux. Don't lecture me," I replied with irritation. "I will work on our current situation, but I need you to let the others know what's going on."

"Silas *isn't* going to be pleased, Tate."

"I know...just, do what you can." The situation had been draining my mind, exhausting me. I had been here for years trying to sort this, and though back home it hadn't been as long, I was looking to get back more than anyone. I hated the mortal realm, and yet it always seemed there was no way for me to escape it no matter how much I wanted to.

"Okay, I'll handle things. Just try and get her on your side. If any of this is going to work, we have to have her willing to help. Or it will all be for nothing."

Hitting the end button, I stood in silence. I looked up at the sky, trying to determine what I was going to do next. I needed Taylor's help, but if she didn't know what she was, there was no way for her to help me.

There was no way for any of this to work without the Elder Hallow.

<u>Taylor</u>

I couldn't pack fast enough. Three suitcases and two duffle bags later, I had managed to get everything important packed into my car. Including a large amount of cash I would use to get situated while I waited for the heat on me to die down.

I wasn't going to risk going back home, but I did have other places I could go hide out. Places I often went to on vacation or when the hunger was becoming too much and I was risking jeopardizing everything that I had built. None of that mattered now.

Once everything was loaded into my car, I went around to the driver's door, ready to drive away. Stopping, I felt eyes watching me. Turning to look over my shoulder, I gazed into the darkness. My eyes struggled to adjust as I tried to see if any figures lurked within the shadows and were a risk to me.

Nothing.

The eerie silence that filled the surrounding area was more than I could take, almost suffocating. The hairs on the back of my neck stood up. An uneasiness swished in the pit of my stomach. Not wasting another second, I jumped into my car, slamming the door and locking it behind me. Pushing my keys into the ignition, I put the car in reverse, and drove down the road to safety.

It wasn't until I was a good few miles away that my racing heart slowed. The only light around me was from my car's headlights, casting a dim light upon the shadowy treelines that passed by my windows.

The place I was going was a cabin I owned within the woods. It was about a two-hour drive from where I lived, but it was so far into the vast wilderness I wouldn't have to worry about anything.

The only thing that I'd ever come in contact with were a few wolf shifters who happened to have a pack nearby, but I was fine with them. We had an understanding, and the Alpha knew who I was. He was actually indebted to me after I had saved his mate's life.

Back when there were no issues. Not real ones, anyway.

It's not like it was back in the day where the only kind of issue anyone had to really worry about was territory. And even then, it was the shifters who worried about that. The pack I had grown accustomed to was peaceful. Its Alpha was a kind man who had seen what the future could possibly be like and chose to create something better.

We hadn't talked in years, but that never mattered. When we saw each other, we picked up like old friends. We only had two rules for our friendship. One, I wouldn't sleep with or feed from anyone in his pack. And two, he would keep my presence a secret no matter who came looking.

I looked forward to seeing him and his fellow pack members. Even though heading back to this particular cabin caused a rush of emotions to flow through me. Memories good and bad, and ones that for years I had refused to confront.

Reaching over to the stereo, I turned it on, letting the music flow through the speakers. I desperately wanted to drown out my thoughts and try to focus on the task ahead. Yet, no matter how hard I tried, there was one thought that kept coming back to my mind.

Tatum and his gorgeous blue eyes.

No matter how delicious he was, he knew about me. About the Elder Hallow and the secrets I was keeping. That wasn't something that someone like him would just let go.

Perhaps with this distance, it would be enough to throw them all off. To have them forget about what I was and their task of finding me. If I were really lucky, he would forget about the Hallow too.

Part of me wondered if that was wishful thinking.

CHAPTER SEVEN

A few hours later, I pulled down the dirt road that led through the winding Evergreen trees. Beneath the canopies, a small cottage was worn down by years of abandonment. Small valleys of the shingled roof and the moss-covered stone chimney greeted me. My heart ached as I grew closer, tears filling my eyes as every memory flooded into me.

This was Deidra's cabin.

A woman who was far from anything I had ever met. The first true friend I had ever really had. She had taught me many things, but most of all, she taught me to love myself again.

She taught me that in order to love others, I had to love myself.

I had to forgive myself for the bad things I had done.

And I did. I forgave myself. And became something more.

I remembered the day she was taken from me. A group of mercenaries murdered her. Some human and others shifters. That day haunted my mind more than anything. I didn't know why they were there or what they wanted, but it was clear that their intentions weren't good.

Especially when Deidra's wards refused them entry.

I had tried so hard to put this memory behind me, to put that day behind me. However, it didn't matter how much I tried to forget the pain over losing her, over that night. It always came back to haunt me.

I could have saved her...I could have done more than I did, but I lost control of myself and because I did, she died.

Along my travels over the years, I'd made friends with various different creatures, and the witches were always my favorite. They had taught me enchantments, spells, things that I could use to protect myself. And the most important thing I learned was from Deidra. She taught me to create wards—or invisible shields—that would protect my home or simply just me.

Something useful for a succubus on the run.

Even one who was completely useless at times. The constant reminder of my mother and sisters negative remarks about how I was a disgrace to the succubi name because I couldn't condone the simplest of things. Like feeding from humans then killing them.

My car pulled into the small clearing in the front of the cabin while a sob crept from my throat. I had swore for years I would never come back to this place. That I wouldn't ever let myself feel the way I had once before yet, here I was.

Even though I felt so much pain, glimpses of happy memories were everywhere I looked. Laughter, love, dancing naked in the rain kind of shit. Memories imprinted, not just in my mind, but in my heart. The house was far from perfect, and it looked condemned to most. However, that was the magic behind this place. The moment I set the wards, it would change, be restored.

That was what Deidra had told me.

Checking my surroundings, I took a deep breath and made my way from the car. My fingers grasped the charm around my neck as I bolted straight for the porch. The wood steps creaked beneath my weight as I searched for the blue pot that held the ruins to this property.

Once I found it, a surge of Deidra's power that remained touched me like an old friend. I pulled the black velvet bag from its hiding spot and turned it over within my hand.

Grasping the stones tightly, I held them to my chest and inhaled the night air. "I'm home, Deidra."

My whispered words went on deaf ears since I was alone. To think I was back in the place where my old life died and my new life began was something I had never considered would happen. The soft night breeze blew gently over my skin, and I opened my eyes, imagining that it was Deidra responding. That it was she who welcomed me home.

I fiddled with my necklace, quickly snatching it off and letting the charm fall into my hand. The smooth red and black marble coloring mesmerized me as it had all those years ago. I knew damn well what would happen the moment I reunited it with its siblings of the black velvet bag.

Safety would fall upon the cabin in a fifty-foot radius. A blast of magical energy would let any magical creature within a two mile area know that I was back. That Deidra's magic was alive again, even if her mortal body was not. Afterall, I was the only one who could activate her magic. The only one who could wield what she left.

That thought made my breath catch in my throat as I held back the emotions threatening to flood through me of the night she died and was taken from me.

I turned towards the altar Deidra had created on the wooden porch, the crystals of old and the love of new still as it was the day I left. Ribbons and bones, jars of magical properties—offerings to the gods as she would call it. Everything was still exactly where she left it. Though time had definitely worn it down.

Picking up a few of the objects that had fallen over, I let my fingers run over a piece of white ribbon before turning my gaze towards the offering plate that was at the center of the altar. My eyes landed upon the Cerulean blue crystal. The crystal's center was hollow with blue and green sparks of life sparkling within the moonlight, as if welcoming me home.

As if speaking to the magic within me.

A magic I fought so hard to ignore, no matter how hard it tried to make itself known.

"Protect me, Dee-dee," I whispered. "Revoke those with evil intent and protect those who seek your guidance. Let your blessing and peace wash over these lands once more."

My words held strong meaning. The moment I dropped the stones of the velvet bag into the crystal altar's center, a surge of power ran through me. It hummed within the air, begging me to complete my offering. All that was left was the ruin in my other hand, the ruin that Deidra said would help me to discover myself.

My heart beat in time to the soft breeze that swayed through the shaded trees. My hand extended forward as I slowly dropped the ruin into the crystal bowl with the others. A wave of calmness washed over me as the ward settled around the cabin.

I was safe now, or at least for the time being.

Panic coursed through me as my gaze cast around the cabin, watching as Deidra scurried around, placing enchantments. Long hair hung in waves over her shoulders, her light green dress flowed around her, hitting every piece of furniture she passed.

"Deidra?" I called out, but it was as if she couldn't hear me. As if I was there but also wasn't. "Deidra!" I called out again, realizing what was happening.

"No. Oh my god, no!"

It was pointless trying to reason with her. Her eyes shifted towards me with a soft forgiving smile. My heart began to break. "I will always be with you, Taylor."

Those words. I remembered those words, and with them, I broke. "Please, don't. Don't walk out that door, Deidra. Don't leave me."

Tears flowed over my cheeks, my breath stuttering as anxiety flowed within me, a raging river only growing stronger with every passing second. Deidra walked out of the front door, and I couldn't hold back. I stormed out behind her. The sounds of gunfire, and the roars of beasts echoed through the woods around us.

The bodies of men and beasts before me clashed into a fight for life and death. Claws slashing and gunfire ringing. The heavy smell of blood in the air I would never be able to forget.

They were here, but it wasn't for each other.

No, they were here for something else. Because the moment that dark-haired man in the distance caught sight of Deidra moving through the chaos in front of me, he yelled for her.

It was clear she was in danger, but she didn't stop what she was doing. I didn't understand what was happening until the dark-haired man ran towards her while another shadowed figure stepped out from the smoke filled air, a gunshot ringing out in the air as I watched her slowly turn towards me with wide eyes, mouthing the word run.

The scream that ripped through my throat was unlike anything I had ever felt before. Every bit of pain and anger I held radiated through me until nothing was left but the shattered pieces of my broken heart.

Jolting upright, I glanced around. My heart beat out of my chest and my face was slick with tears. "It was just a dream..." I muttered, wiping the wetness from my cheeks and trying to calm my racing mind.

It had been so long since that dream plagued me. So long since I had to relieve the night Deidra was taken from me.

The morning sun rose over the treeline, filtering through the window with dust particles dancing within the rays. I wasn't sure how long I had slept but it didn't feel long enough. Wiping my face again, I took a deep breath, raising my eyes to the ceiling as I tried to collect myself.

It was hard to escape my past, but I could try to make the best of a bad situation. Even if it came with the pain of my past.

It didn't matter what I did in life. I was going to have to come to terms with the fact I was going to be hunted. I wasn't quite sure why I was being hunted, but I had a feeling it had to do with whatever happened the night Deidra was killed.

My mind drifted back to Tatum—the hunter who saved me—and his gorgeous smile, and sexy broad shoulders...*oh, for fuck's sake, I had to get laid.*

As much as I wanted to continue being wary of him, and I was, something about last night when he was at my place felt familiar. As if I was supposed to trust him, and yet it didn't make any sense. He had asked about the Hallow. He had known about one of the most secret aspects of my life, something no one should know about.

A sigh left my lips, and I reached over to grab my phone from the nightstand, checking the time. Half past ten in the morning. I hadn't slept this late in so long. Every part of me wanted to lay in bed all day, wallowing in my own self pity, but the low whistling of someone familiar caused a small smile to creep across my face. If I was going to be forced to hide out here, the least I could do was make time for old friends.

"Logan..." His name came out a whisper as I swung my legs over the edge of the bed. Darting from the small bedroom through the cabin towards the front door.

Behind the wards, I was protected, even from Logan, who wasn't a welcome guest here.

He and I were friends, but Deidra didn't trust him.

I stepped onto the porch where four wolves and a gray-haired man stepped forward from beneath the canopies of the trees. "Logan, you aged well."

Moving closer to the ward, a deep heartiness reverberated from his chest as his eyes scanned over the magical force field, his hand hovering inches above as he seemed to admire it. "I take it you're in trouble again?"

I shrugged with a meek smile. "Define trouble."

"All those years ago, I thought you had finally been claimed and weren't coming back," he replied with a sly grin shaking his head. "I should have known better."

"Claimed?" I replied in a joking tone. "You and I both know that isn't what happened the night I left."

Nodding his head, he sighed heavily. I knew he remembered that night because he was the one who aided in my escape from the madness. Back then he was a young man barely in his prime. A man hesitant about helping me because he wanted to protect his new mate and the pack he had been left in charge of.

However, over time, he was able to put that hesitation behind him. Deidra, having brought us closer together. Helping to build the friendship that I thought we still had, but right now...I could see the same unease in his eyes that he had when I first met him.

As if he wasn't sure whether or not to trust me, and I could understand that. The night that Deidra died, we all lost a part of ourselves, and Logan lost even more. His wolves had helped to defend us, and a vast majority from what I heard later on had been killed.

I tried to make amends with him back then, months after the event. However, back then, he made it clear that he felt it was best that I didn't come back. That I found a new future somewhere else.

"I know what you mean," he finally added. "I suppose I was just hoping that you had been able to make something of the new life you were so eager to have. You know that's what she would have wanted."

She.

Deidra.

I didn't want to hear the comment, but I knew he was saying it out of kindness. Friend to friend.

"Life isn't always as easy as we would hope," I called out, trying to maintain my composure. "Is that why your pack is in their wolf?"

Glancing at his pack members, he gestured for them to go. Two of them listened, but the other two shifted. Their bones cracking and echoing through the air caused me to cringe. I knew it was part of their nature, but something about the sound made me dizzy with nausea.

"Don't tell me that still bothers you?" He laughed, noticing my unease.

Choking back my disgust, I forced a smile. "Yeah...you could have warned me."

"Where would the fun be in that?"

My eyes admired the two gorgeous figures of his beta and gamma in their full naked glory. Roaming up and down their tattooed bronze colored skin, I took in every curve of their muscles that dipped down into the 'V' like structure that accented their well-defined cocks.

Clearing my throat, my eyes fell to their faces. Grins spread across their lips as the gamma crossed his arms over his chest, flaunting off his body as if to say 'look at me'. "So, why are you guys on alert? I thought things were better out here."

"It's been years, Taylor," Adam, Logan's beta, called out. "You're still as gorgeous as I remember."

Cheeky fuck.

"Always the charmer, Adam. Tell me, how's your *mate*...what was her name? *Megan*?"

His eyes widened at the mention of her name. The woman who about killed him when she found out we fucked right before they got together. He was a special case back then. A wolf who had lost his first mate, and had no clue he could have a second. Even Deidra had enjoyed him with me, which was a memory for another time.

"She's great," Logan replied. "In fact, she will be happy to know you're back."

Adam's gaze snapped back to Logan with shock as Logan, and his gamma laughed. I wasn't sure what was going on, but a few choice words from Adam seemed to cause him to panic further.

"Oh, I'd love to see her. Tell her about our *naked* reunion, no? I mean, you were always a sucker for the way my—"

"Okay!" he shouted, his face turning red from embarrassment. "Let's just...not tell her please."

"Alright, alright." Logan smiled. "Let's get back to business. All I want to know is if the hunters are after you. The last thing I need is my pack being put into danger, Taylor."

His comment had me freezing in place. Nothing could keep away the reality lingering in the background, waiting for me.

"Um, no." They weren't technically after me, so saying no wouldn't be a lie, but there was somebody seeking my help. I just wouldn't call that being hunted.

Logan narrowed his gaze, crossing his arms over his chest as if calculating my words. I was never great at lying, and I hoped he bought what I said. The last thing I wanted was an issue between him and me.

"Is that right? I heard Salem was in some trouble of the murderous-kind. None of that had to deal with you?"

My lips parted slightly at his question, and I sighed. "Well, I mean, I believe there was an issue with a bear shifter last night, but it had nothing to do with me. I just decided to get out of there because I didn't want anyone looking at me. You know I like keeping to myself."

Nodding, he glanced at Adam, who had a brow raised at my comment. "She isn't lying."

Thank god...

"Very well," Logan replied, happy with Adam's assessment.

Adam always had a unique gift for being able to tell if people were lying. I wasn't sure if the ward helped stop his gift or if he did know I lied, but was choosing to not say anything. Regardless, I was happy they believed me.

Until Logan's eyes snapped to the space behind me, a low growl emitting from his throat that made my heart jump. "We're not alone."

Looking towards the area he stared at, I watched the shadowed figure of a man step forth, followed by two wolves, and my heart dropped into my stomach.

Fuck...you've got to be kidding me.

CHAPTER EIGHT

<u>Tatum</u>

The sun peeked over the horizon, causing birds and other critters to come to life. Shadows from the forest slowly disappeared, fading to rest beneath the canopies. I had followed Taylor from her apartment, something I wasn't ashamed of. There was no way after all this time of searching for her that I was going to risk her slipping through my fingers.

Sitting from where I'd slept on the ground, I stretched my arms above my head and stood to my feet. I realized quickly I was no longer alone in the woods. My eyes cast towards the cabin to see the front door slowly opening.

I could have gone in there last night, crossed her wards and finished our conversation. They were impressive, but they weren't enough to keep someone like me out. Even if I did admire her for trying to protect herself.

At the end of the night, though, she needed time to process. And I'd respect her enough to give her a night for that.

"Finally, she's awake," I muttered, watching her take one slow step after another until she seemed to spot what she was looking for—something at the back of the cabin caught her attention. From the shadows of the trees on the far side of her, a man stepped out, and he wasn't alone.

I wasn't sure why seeing her so happy over this man burned an itch within me, but I stood there regardless—watching.

There was still so much that I could learn from her. So much that I could take in before I confronted her. Which was going to have to be soon, considering the texts from my brother didn't stop coming in last night until early hours of the morning.

He knew how important she was and what she could do.

The distance between me and them prevented me from understanding what they were talking about. Which only fueled my irritation and interest over this situation. I wanted to get closer, to make myself known, but it wouldn't end well if she knew I was here.

The cracking of branches behind me piqued my attention, picking up the sound of approaching footsteps, letting me know my time of being hidden was up. As much as I didn't want her to know I was here, I wasn't going to have a choice. The wolves had found me. I wasn't worried about what was going to happen next, but irritated I couldn't have a moment longer to admire her.

"Don't. Your leader will be fine with my presence. There is no need to cause a scene," I said clearly, knowing full well the two wolves who approached behind understood.

Turning to face them, their peppered gray pelts made them great at hiding in the shadows, but their Alpha really did need to train them better on being stealthy. Letting out a heavy sigh, I pushed one hand in my pocket and gestured with my other towards the direction of the Alpha.

"By all means, lead the way."

The conversation with Taylor, myself, and the Alpha was surely going to be interesting. She thought I was a hunter, even though I tried to explain that I wasn't. And the Alpha, though unsure of who it was in these parts, had more than likely heard of who my family was.

Step by step, I made my way towards the others. Taylor's eyes met mine with shock in their depths. It was clear she wasn't expecting to see me. Why would she? She thought she could get away, and I wouldn't find her. But I did. And from now on, I always would.

She was protected behind her ward, and she looked uncertain about my appearance at her getaway home. Not that I would blame her. I'm sure it was overwhelming when she tried so hard to avoid me.

"What are you doing here, stranger?" The man's words were cut short as I got closer to him. The men at his side stood their ground, all of whom were naked. For a group of men trying to act bold, it wasn't exactly intimidating.

"You're one of the—" the Alpha replied softly. My eyes met his, watching as they grew wider with realization. He recognized me. Wouldn't have been the first time another wolf shifter did.

"I am."

The blunt reply caused the men to all glance at each other. The beta and gamma backed away slowly as a sign of respect.

"What are you doing here?" the Alpha asked, confusion littering his face.

There was no way I was going to tell him why I was really here, but as I let my eyes slide from him to where Taylor stood, I smiled. "For her."

Taylor narrowed her gaze, her plump pink lips parted before she quickly snapped her lips closed with a frown. "You're a—"

"—friend," I quickly said. "A friend trying to help you, but I think we got off to the wrong start in our last conversation. Which is why I came to continue it. To clear up any confusion regarding my offer."

I didn't care if the Alpha and his pack believed me. I was here for one reason and one reason only. If these wolves thought that they could take me on, they would be sadly mistaken. I stood there staring at Taylor, not allowing my gaze to break from hers as I awaited for her to give me some type of reassurance that we could talk. All the while, I knew quite well the Alpha and his wolves were staring at the two of us as if waiting for something.

Whatever they were waiting for, I wasn't quite sure. But I had a feeling they were going to take their leave soon. Which did end up happening when I cleared my throat, turning my gaze back to the Alpha with a pointed look as to say he needed to leave us alone.

Nodding his head, he turned his attention to Taylor. "I can see that the two of you need to catch up. If you need me, you know how to get a hold of me."

He backed away with his right and left hand. The three of them disappeared with the two other wolves who had sought me out in the woods. I had a feeling that they wouldn't leave entirely. Simply keep watch from a distance, but that was fine. It didn't matter and when they were out of sight, I turned my attention back to her.

An angry scowl graced her face as she crossed her arms over her chest, shaking her head. "I can't believe you found me here. How did you find me?"

"Well, you weren't very subtle when you left for one."

She scoffed, rolling her eyes as she turned away, making her way back towards the cabin. "Well, you're free to leave. I have nothing to discuss with you."

"Oh, but I think you do."

Stopping in her tracks, she turned to glance at me from over her shoulder. "No, I don't. I don't know what the fuck you think you're going to get from me, but I can promise you it will be nothing."

Stubborn. That was the only word I could think to describe her as. It didn't matter she knew deep down we needed to discuss things, she simply ignored it. Her own selfish will to act like I didn't exist taking over. And no matter how gorgeous she was, it was becoming irritating.

"Why don't we stop with the bullshit, princess. I don't have time for it. We can either talk now, or I can come in there and talk to you. The choice is yours."

Her mouth hung open, and her eyes were wide with shock before laughter escaped her. "I hate to break it to you, but you can't get in here, and I don't have to sit and talk to you about anything. So you can stay here if you want, but I'm going inside."

She turned as if she thought that was going to be the end of the conversation. Watching every move she made towards the front door, I enjoyed the sight of her perky ass sway side to side. "Alright then...inside it is," I muttered, stepping forward and easily passing the ward, which caused her to gasp in disbelief as she looked over at me.

"No fucking way—"

"As I was saying...we need to talk," I replied, cutting her off before she could continue.

I could see in her eyes she wanted to run. But it was her rebellious nature she tried to ignore that caused her to stay. Instead of rushing her, I moved slowly towards the house. One of her hands was on the doorknob, the other quickly covering her lips as she looked at me with defiance and fear.

"How is this possible? Deidra's wards..." she muttered softly.

"They are remarkable," I replied, stopping only feet from her on the porch as I looked around the area, taking in the altar that held the wards together. "However, they don't work on me because I'm not here to hurt you...nor am I human."

"What do you mean, you're not human?"

Shrugging my shoulders, I let a grin cross my lips as I clasped my hands in front of me. "I mean that I'm not."

"What are you then? I can always tell what a supernatural is—" Again, she closed up quickly. She hadn't meant to say that, but I found it interesting she had. It must have been one of the gifts the Hallow gave her. Something I would have to let my sister know about later.

"You don't have to hide things from me, Taylor. I'm not going to hurt you. I'm here to help you as I have said multiple times."

"Okay," she whispered. "As long as you swear that you're not going to hurt me, I'll listen to what you have to say. But I can't help you with the Hallow."

I stared at her knowing that she could, but not wanting to press the issue when she was finally giving me a chance to explain what was going on.

"Okay," I replied. She turned, opening the door to her cabin, and gestured for me to follow.

Stepping inside, I was surprised by how new everything looked compared to the outside of the cabin. Outside, it was dilapidated as if the house was crumbling. However, inside white paint was fresh. Yellow touches of color gave it an airy feeling, almost like the home my mother used to keep.

Seeing the touches that reminded me of my mother brought me back to the night that I lost her. The night where I was changed from a boy into a man, and forced to live with the realization that I would no longer have her there to guide me, to reassure me that everything was going to be alright.

Flowers littered every surface and seemed fresh as if they had been there forever, grown into the home when I knew damn well that wasn't the case.

"The home is spelled..."

It wasn't a question, but more of a statement that she seemed to recognize. "Yeah, it is."

A lost, almost distant look flashed in her eyes as she glanced around the home with a hint of a smile on her face. What I wouldn't give to know what was going through her mind. This woman—though my charge—was far more beautiful than any woman I had ever seen.

Her age was not reflected physically but was given away within the depths of her eyes. Succubi were known to live a long time as long as they fed. Which shocked me because she was adamant multiple times she wasn't a killer. I wondered how she stayed so young when she never killed her prey.

"Well, shall we begin?"

CHAPTER NINE

<u>Taylor</u>

I didn't know what to expect when I agreed to let Tatum come inside my home. Not that I had a choice. The moment he crossed the ward with ease, I thought I was seeing things. I had watched the ward throw men who tried to cross illegally, hundreds of yards away.

Tatum walked through it as if it was not even there.

"There are things about what I'm doing that may sound confusing, but I want you to hear me out before you just shoot down what I'm saying."

"Okay," I replied. It was clear it didn't matter where I tried to run, he was going to find me. The only thing I could do was hope that when I finished listening to him, he would respect me when I said no and asked him to leave.

Taking a deep breath, I stared at him, our eyes locked, as a sense of determination seemed to flow over him as he nodded and continued on.

"I'm not from here, Taylor," he started, his eyes focused on me with a seriousness I wasn't expecting. "I was sent here a long time ago to find a source of power that could help my family. Well, not just my family but entire realms. A source of power never meant to be in the mortal world. The moment I met you in your shop, Taylor, I knew you were different."

Raising a brow, I frowned. "Different?"

"Yes," he nodded. "You're different. I could read your aura."

This wasn't the first time someone had told me I was different, but it was definitely the first time someone said they could read my aura, and the way Tatum was going about this was getting cornier by the second. "So you're a stalker?"

"Yes—wait no," he groaned, stumbling over his words. "I'm not a stalker."

Leaning back on the sofa, I scoffed. "Really? Because you could have fooled me."

"Will you stay on topic please." He sighed. "What I'm trying to tell you is important."

"Okay, so tell me. Stop drawing out the situation with a long story."

I appreciated his approach in trying to give me a back story, but I didn't want it. I was more of the "get to the point" kind of girl. My life—a seemingly disastrous mess—had no time for long drawn out stories.

Tate, however, didn't seem pleased by my defiant remark. He scowled before tilting his head from side to side, cracking his neck. "As I was saying, I knew you were supernatural. I just didn't know what exactly until I saw what you did in the alley."

My body went rigid the moment he mentioned the alley. I hadn't meant to go completely out of sorts but the anger of the shifter attacking me forced me to use powers that I wasn't always able to control.

"I see," I muttered, gesturing for him to continue.

Surprised by my willingness to listen, he smiled and relaxed a bit. "Okay...well, you're a celestial creature, Taylor. You are the Elder Hallow secret that your family has been protecting. You were stolen hundreds of years ago from the Arcane Gateway."

"I'm sorry, the what?"

"That Arcane Gateway," he replied, as if he didn't understand why I asked. "It's located at the Phoenix Temple. A sacred place that was protected for thousands of years by supernaturals of all kinds. There they protected the Elder Hallow. The balance between life and death."

The silence that fell between us was deafening. My lips parted, my mouth wide-open as I soaked in what he said. There was no way that ANY of that made sense. I wasn't the Hallow, and I had no idea what an Arcane Gateway was or what he meant by me being a Celestial. This man was clearly fucking delusional, and I wanted no part in that.

"Okay…" I burst out laughing as I stood to my feet. My mind raced a mile a minute as I began pacing around the living room. He was being utterly ridiculous, and if he thought I was going to believe any of this bullshit… he was sadly mistaken.

"Hmm, you're taking this better than I thought."

My eyes found his again as I furrowed them in disbelief. I had given him a chance to tell me something truthful, and instead he made up the shit he just spewed. Maybe this man was actually a hunter who had gone off the radar and was missing from one of those crazy houses.

Regardless, he irritated me. From the relaxed way that he lounged upon the loveseat to the cool glance in his gaze, I couldn't believe he was being serious. I wasn't sure entirely how to take what he said, and the fact he was so cool and collected when telling me as if he had spoken about this a million times kind of caught me off guard, but brought me amusement.

This was what he had wanted to tell me. This was what all of this shit from the moment I had met him had been about? Tatum had completely lost his mind. If he thought there was any way I was to believe him.

Astonishment filled me as I tried to formulate words, my mouth opening slightly as a small scoff left my throat while I shook my head.

"Taking it better..." Laughter left me. "If you think I believe any of what the hell you just said, you're out of your fucking mind."

I was exhausted with his presence and everything else I had gone through since I met him. Stopping, I started to consider what I had just gone over in my head.

Since the moment I met him...he had been looking for me?

"Did you...has all that's happened to me over the last few weeks been because of you?!" I practically snapped at him. It was the only thing that made sense, because despite those gorgeous azure eyes looking back at me, he was a stranger.

Tatum stared at me with annoyance marred into his face, his fist clenched upon his knee. An expression of disapproval flared within his eyes. Sure, he had said many times he was here to help me, but that didn't mean a damn thing. I didn't know him, and the fact that my perfect life seemed to tip upside down right after meeting him, it couldn't have been a coincidence.

"No, Taylor," he replied in a dark monotone voice as if trying to keep his composure. "If I wanted to cause you problems or ruin your life, I would have. Are you always this difficult when it comes to people trying to help you? I don't understand why you keep acting the way you are."

His questioning and scolding me, wondering why I'm defensive, annoyed me. However, there was no point in trying to figure him out. I was done with the conversation.

"You came and said what you had to say, Tatum. I think it's time for you to leave," I said coldly, walking towards the front door. The sooner he left, the better.

"No," he replied as my hand grasped the door-knob.

Spinning to face him, I frowned. "No? What do you mean, no?"

"I mean no, I'm not leaving." He shrugged, propping his feet up on the sofa, making himself comfortable.

He was seriously making himself comfortable in my home! I mean, I would never do that in his or anyone else's, and yet, there he sat with his legs up, smug expression firm on his face as he reclined.

"I'm sorry, what?"

"What...what?"

"Don't you what...what me, Tatum. What do you mean you're not leaving. We have nothing else to discuss, and this is my home. I would like you to leave," I replied confidently, my head held high as I tried to show him I wasn't going to back down.

However, all it did was cause him to chuckle, completely ignoring my request.

Screaming in frustration, I stormed to my room, slamming the door behind me. "The arrogance of that man!"

"I can hear you..." he called from the living room, pissing me off even further.

"Completely unbelievable. This big buffoon is sooo—gahh!"

<u>Tatum</u>

Working with this woman was like working with a toddler who threw a tantrum when she didn't get her way. I wasn't quite sure what her damn problem was, but I wasn't going to give into her like everyone else probably had in her life. What bothered me the most was she was a succubi, and those women were usually deadly and dangerous. However, her mentality was different as if she had spent too much time in the human world to be able to understand what she was.

That knowledge alone concerned me because what I needed her for was going to be far more dangerous than simply just making sure her shop was taken care of. The almost youthful side to her mind was what perplexed me the most. How a creature as strong as she was was completely oblivious to what she was and who she had to become.

A creature hundreds of years old, who still had the mentality of that of a woman barely into her adulthood. Finn and Silas had told me there was a good chance that she wouldn't remember anything. Especially since she was taken as a child, but I figured something would jog her mind.

Guess I was wrong.

The evening started settling in after a long afternoon of silence. Taylor stayed locked away in her room, refusing to come out, and though I had made myself comfortable on the sofa at one point, I couldn't sit there long. I had to get up, move around, make myself known, try to make myself comfortable, because goddess knows she wasn't welcoming.

Rummaging through the kitchen, I made use of the materials that were there. It was clear nobody had been living here in quite some time. The kitchen was bare save for a few fruits and vegetables that happened to be sitting in baskets upon a counter, which also stunned me because I didn't see a garden or anything like that nearby. It must have been part of the enchantment that the woman, Deidre she called her, had set up in this place long ago.

I was curious how well of a connection she had with the witch. I knew that she had spent quite a bit of time here with her, and that Deidra had been her mentor but I wasn't quite sure how deep their connection really went. Even with the wolves she seemed to have such a good relationship with, which was new to me.

Gazing around the cabin, I had taken in everything there was. My mind relived the night of the battle. The night that so many lives changed...including mine.

Pollux and Silas filled me in where they could at the start of my mission but I was used to them leaving out important details. Details they didn't feel necessary, but oftentimes were. What intrigued me the most though was that out of all the places I could have found her, that I could have traced her back to, she came back to where it all began.

As the sun began to sink across the afternoon sky, casting shadows upon the property, I dived into cooking what was available. The fragrance of the food I found, as well as herbs and spices, flowed through the home, drifting through every single corner. Hopefully, it was enough to pull Taylor from her room.

No matter the situation, I wanted her to come with me willingly. Forcing her to do anything was never going to get her to cooperate in the long run. And I never had considered that this would probably be the most aggravating part of my entire mission.

Growing up with my family, though we had our issues, we worked together, especially after what happened to my sister. We learned our family was different. Our family was expected, among all other supernatural creatures, to take a stance and make things right within the world, within the other supernatural communities.

Balance within the supernatural worlds was extremely important.

Something my family took pride in. We fixed what was broken.

Shuffling footsteps echoed from down the hallway towards the living room where the bedroom was. I was curious if she was going to come see what I was doing. I finished up with what I was doing, plating the food as it was done.

"I see that you're just making yourself at home, in my house," Taylor called ten minutes later from the living room. She appeared around the corridor. Looking up, I caught her mesmerizing eyes and smiled as I glanced down at the pan on the stove.

"I guess you could say that. Now, are you hungry? There's plenty here for both of us."

She hesitated, before nodding her head, making her way to the rickety wooden island where two bar stools were. She pulled one from the side away from where I stood. I respected her wishes and plated the food up, sliding a plate towards her.

"Thank you," she muttered. "You *really* didn't have to go to all this trouble."

I internally chuckled, trying to keep my sarcastic comments about going to trouble to a minimum. She was being polite, that was a first. However, every part of me wanted to mock her about how trouble was all she had brought me since I met her. Though being a dick probably wasn't the best way to end the day.

She was being social without trying to get me to leave. At least that was something. It was better we be cordial to one another while enjoying breakfast together than constantly fighting against one another. Even if I'd rather strangle her for being absolutely stubborn. It was some kind of progress, which meant that I was getting back on the right track of trying to convince her.

To come to my homeland, where she needed to be.

"It's okay. I was starving, and I noticed that you had barely eaten all day, so I figured I would make something.

My phone rang, drawing both of our attention. I pulled it from my pocket, seeing my brother's number across the screen. If he was calling right now, it was because it was important. It was probably because he had been tipped off that hunters were on their way.

No matter the situation, I couldn't let her know. I'd play it cool, and act like everything was okay. I had to get her to trust me, and I had to know more about her.

But most of all, I had to keep her calm until the right moment we had to run.

"Hello?" I answered, waiting for him to give me some spiel about how I was taking too long. The words he said rattled me, and made me realize we had far less time than I thought, much shorter than I could have comprehended to begin with.

"You've been located. Her cabin, whatever, it's been located. You both need to get the fuck out of there. The hunters are on their way right now."

Shit...I knew it.

CHAPTER TEN

<u>**Taylor**</u>

Uncertainty had never been something I was okay with. My sister had often compared me to a skittish cat unable to feel anything but fear for the outside world. A comparison I was never pleased with. However, as the smile on Tatum's face fell and his jaw went rigid, I knew something was wrong. His entire body screamed turmoil, hesitation, and concern. His body tense, his eyes darting to the kitchen window as he cleared his throat hanging up his phone.

"Is something wrong?"

Our eyes meet, Tatum's eyes calculating what he was going to say before letting out a heavy sigh and placing his phone back into his pocket. "How strong are the wards?"

Who the hell answers a question like that?! Panic filtered through me. For a man who seemed to have his shit together since I met him, eager to share information with me to get me to like him, he wasn't doing a good job of it right now.

"What?" I asked, "why does that matter?"

His silence was slightly unsettling as he turned back to me with a smile from where he was cooking on the stove. "No reason. I was just impressed by the magical aspects."

Liar. Deciding to assume he was telling the truth—even though it was against my better judgment—I nodded with a faint smile, trying to show I was satisfied with his answer.

"Oh. Um, they're pretty strong. Never really had issues before. Thanks though..."

He nodded, silence again falling over us that was more annoying than his presence. If he was going to be insistent about being in my safe home, then the least he could do was actually present normal conversation. The man was completely gorgeous for sure, but he made me wonder if he socialized with normal people at all. The brooding front he was giving right now didn't exactly make a girl feel comfortable.

"So...that smells good."

That smells good? God, I was fucking more awkward than him right now.

He turned to me again as he stood before my stove in a pair of khaki shorts that hugged his well sculpted ass and a navy blue shirt that clung to every rippling muscle beneath—my heart raced, just by a single glance. "Yeah, well what's in front of you is only the tipping point of my mastery cooking lessons."

"Mastery cooking lessons?" I questioned with amusement. My eyes drifted towards the plate in front of me taking in the array of colors and the delicious smell.

"Yep, mastery…"

I knew damn well he was trying to share in his humor with me, but I wasn't honestly in the mood for it. "Thanks, but I'm not actually hungry."

Liar. You damn well know you are.

"Okay, that's fine with me," he replied, casting his glance back to the pan on the stove, "so I was thinking…we kind of got off on the wrong foot before. I know that you're not happy with me being here, but I thought perhaps we can talk after. Start over and get to know each other."

Shock was an understatement. I hadn't taken Tatum as the kind of man who would be willing to 'start over' as he called it. I took him more as a 'take charge and demand' kind of person.

Raising a brow I stared at him. "Really?"

"Yeah, why not?" He chuckled, "did you have something else you wanted to do?"

Something else. Like that was even fucking possible. I was stuck behind this ward, and he knew that. My face fell at his comment as I gave him a dumbfounded expression. "As much as I would love to be anywhere else, doing anything else…I can't and you know that."

"Great!" He exclaimed as he gave me a pearly white smile. "That means we will have fun."

I wasn't sure why there was a sudden change to his behavior, but I was fully aware I couldn't continue to be a complete bitch to him. Maybe if he did know me, he would be able to understand why I can't give him what he wants. Or perhaps I was being naive, and this was just a ploy.

Taking a moment, I eye'd the food in the pan biting my bottom lip. "Clean up the kitchen when you're done, and then we can talk."

I didn't actually care about the kitchen, but I needed an excuse of some sort to set boundaries with him. Not to mention I needed a moment to get clarity and space before I actually agreed to do what he was saying.

Turning from the kitchen—no longer interested in the food he was cooking—I made my way through to the living room and out the front door for fresh air. I needed room to breathe, to clear my mind after everything going on. My life hadn't been turned upside down this much in what felt like years and now once again I was thrown into the same loop I had been in before.

I closed the front door behind me and let out a heavy breath, my body going lax as I made my way towards the old rickety porch swing that sat on the far left side of the porch. The paint was chipped after decades of being neglected, and there was no telling by looking at it if it would even support someone's weight.

But I knew otherwise.

The moment I rested upon it, slinging my legs over the side as I reclined back, I closed my eyes and simply listened to the world around me. Even with the ward the birds and animals of the forest were able to still come and go. The ward only kept out supernatural aspects, and those who would issue to harm me.

It was peaceful out here, a sort of peace that made someone consider never going back to civilization—or more so made me consider never going back.

Out here, my family didn't know where I was. Hell, the world didn't.

Yet, staying in solitary never happened for long. Something always threw me back into the land of the living. Something about this world always seemed to try, and call me home.

However, with my family out of the picture for right now—I didn't have to worry about being reprimanded for the way I chose to live my life. I was able to simply be me, and being me—an introvert in a forced extrovert world—I found solace in the silence.

My gifts were dulled by being alone. And that meant my heart wasn't constantly racing every two minutes at every sound that would make me wonder if it was time for me to run. A feeling I had grown to loathe over the years.

The creek of the front screen door opened, catching my attention. My eyes opened quickly as I darted to Tatum as he came out the front door with a bowl of food in his hand and a smile on his face. The same smile that made my stomach flutter but also annoyed me.

As if he knew something I didn't and took amusement in that.

"I was wondering where you ran off too."

Slowly sitting up I curled my legs under me as I watched him closely. No matter if he said he wasn't here to hurt me, I wasn't going to believe him so easily. There was something he was hiding. A secret he didn't want me to know, and knowing that was enough to keep me on my guard. Because so far the only truths that had come from his mouth were that of half truths.

"I needed to clear my mind," I admitted as he took a seat on an old stool near where I was sitting on the swing. "I'd be careful sitting there... It might break."

"No, it won't." He chuckled.

He wasn't wrong, it wouldn't. But I was hoping he wouldn't know that and would find somewhere else to get comfortable. "You never know... just wanted you to be aware."

His blue eyes met mine one more as his smile widened before he shook his head and dove fork deep into his food. "If you say so. Well, the kitchen is clean, so I guess we can start getting to know one another."

Damn, he just jumped right into shit didn't he?

"Uh, okay..." I muttered, glancing away. My eyes searched the forest as if expecting someone to be standing there, lurking within the shadows of the canopies watching us. "What do you want to know?"

"Hmm... maybe we should start with the basics?"

The basics. That wasn't a lot of information to go off of. There was an array of topics that I could fucking go into, but that didn't mean I wanted to. Thinking for a moment, a sarcastic thought came to mind as I let the corner of my lip twitch, turning my gaze back to Tatum.

"Well, if you want to go back to basics, I guess we can. But I figured a man of your age would already know."

He frowned at my comment, "what do you mean by that?"

Shrugging my shoulders, I turned to face him more. "I mean ,I thought everyone learned this at a young age... where babies come from. I mean, I have no issue with—"

"Whoa what?" He gasped, almost choking on his food as he stared at me in shock. Laughter erupted from my throat at his expression. "That's not what I was talking about, and you know it."

"I don't know, actually. I don't know you or where you're from. I don't know why you have been following me other than the small bit of shit you have spewed since I met you, and honestly, you haven't exactly given me a reason to believe you or trust you. So when you say you want to start from the beginning... I have no idea what you mean."

Tatum stared at me for a moment in silence, my words seemingly sinking in before he sighed, placing his fork in the bowl and then the bowl on the ground at his feet. His hands clasped before him as he leaned forward on his knees. "Okay, you have a point."

Damn, admitting I'm right... that's a first.

"So—?" I replied, waiting for something further.

"So, let's fix that. How about we play a game. Twenty-one questions, you ask me one and vice versa. Does that sound okay?"

I knew what he was talking about as I had done that sort of ice-breaker before. "Fine, I'll go first though."

Nodding his head, he picked up his bowl again, "okay. Shoot."

"You said you weren't from here. So, where are you from?" That was a basic question, one he shouldn't have an issue with answering, but he did hesitate for a moment before opening his mouth.

"So, that's a bit of a loaded question. Originally, I'm from Idaho. Some of my family still resides there, but my more fixed location is in a place called Lenar."

"Lenar? Where is that located... I've never heard of it."

"Uh, huh." He laughed, shaking his head, "a question for a question. I answered yours now it's my turn."

Rolling my eyes, I nodded, "fine. Ask your question."

I was wary of what he was going to ask. My heart raced a little faster at the thought of him asking about the hallow again, but to my surprise he went a different direction.

"Do you not get along with your family?"

"That's a bit forward, don't you think?" I shot back, not having been prepared for something of that stature.

"It's just a question," he shrugged.

Taking a deep breath, I thought about my family. My sister, the chaotic mess, constantly trying to prove she is better than me by kissing my mother's ass. And my mother, the supreme leader of my fucked up family. Both of them, a stain on my existence.

"Not exactly," I finally muttered. "Is it that obvious?"

"I mean, yeah." He replied in a nonchalant kind of way. "You kind of chose to come out here instead of to them when shit got bad. So it was kind of obvious."

If he had only known the truth of what really went on with my family he would better understand why I didn't go to them. They were a pain, and not only that they judged me at every turn trying to show me that I didn't know how to live my life. That my only choice was to be loyal to them and do what my mother said.

Something I refused to do.

"I take it you're close with your family then?"

Nodding his head, he gave me a weak smile. "Yeah for the most part. My eldest sister and I are the closest though. She actually saved my life when I was little."

Before I could open my mouth again to comment on his statement, a sense of panic washed over me. My eyes went wide as I jumped to my feet, scanning the surrounding woods as terror set in. There were people out there, people who weren't welcome and the magic of my home sensed it.

"What's wrong, Taylor?" Tatum quickly asked as he jumped to his feet beside me.

"Someone's out there... someone that isn't friendly."

"Shit..." he replied, causing me to turn to him. "I thought we would have more time."

I couldn't believe it. "What the fuck do you mean you thought we had more time?!"

Shaking his head he grabbed my hand dropping the bowl to the ground as he tried to pull me behind him back into the house. "We have to go."

"No!" I exclaimed, ripping my hand from his while trying to ignore the way his touch felt against my skin. "What the fuck are you hiding?! You said you wanted us to try and get to know each other and now what... you have people here to get me?"

"No, damnit." He snapped at me, his body moving closer to mine causing my breath to catch in my throat. "I'm trying to protect you from the people who are trying to kill you. I have been looking for you for so long, Taylor. I don't have time to play childish games anymore. If we don't leave now your good as dead. Now for once, please stop fighting me and let me protect you like I was sent here to fucking do."

Taken back by his outburst, my heart thumping within my chest I took in what he said. Every part of me was screaming to run the other way, but I also didn't want to. I wanted to trust him, and honestly I had nothing left to lose. Nodding my head, my eyes latching on to his outstretched hand I did the last thing I ever expected.

I let my guard down and took his hand. Praying to whatever god was out there that I hadn't just signed my own life away. "Okay... but if I die, I'm going to haunt you forever."

A chuckle left him as his hand smoothed over the back of my own, "I wouldn't expect less princess."

CHAPTER ELEVEN

Unfortunate circumstances didn't even touch our current situation as I gave my life over to a man I barely knew, hoping he would get me out of the woods alive. A normal person would have called me insane. Even perhaps questioned my will to live. However, I was living on the edge. Something I never did.

"What are we going to do?" I asked as he pulled me into the house, locking the door behind us as if that was going to keep them out.

"Just...give me a minute."

I wasn't new to running from danger, nor was I new to fighting off danger. But I felt as if neither would be beneficial at that moment. A loud boom echoed through the home, shaking the walls. My eyes widened in shock as I turned towards the window, watching as the ward shook around my home.

"They're trying to break the ward," I muttered, watching the ward shake again. Never had I seen a display like this before, and I suddenly wondered if Deidra's magic would actually hold.

A firm grasp on my upper arm pulled me back from my internal dilemma. Cool blue eyes stared down at me as I waited for Tatum to tell me what we were doing.

"We have to go, Taylor. When I tell you to run, I want you to run."

"Wait," I gasped as he pulled me towards the back door. "Where the hell am I running to? I mean, where are we going? Surely they have this place surrounded."

Laughter escaped him as he nodded. "Yeah, I'm sure they do. However, they won't be able to see you."

Furrowing my brow, I tried to understand what he meant. There was no time for further explanations as his lips crashed upon me, taking my breath away. A moan rumbled in my throat as a wave of electric fire seemed to rush across my skin. My heart raced as a tingle of desire pooled between my thighs, wanting him to fuck me till I couldn't stand.

The feeling was fleeting as he pulled away from me. Breathless panting escaped us both as he cleared his throat, obviously having felt the exact same thing I did as he turned his eyes towards the window outside. "You will have fifteen minutes, Taylor. Head south to the road. I have a car hidden by the side of it. I will meet you there."

"You're not coming with me?" I whispered as his blue eyes met mine once more.

"I'll be right behind you."

The smile upon his lips made my heart skip a beat. However, I was taken aback and confused by what the hell had possessed the man to kiss me in the first place. Deciding that right now probably wasn't the time to question him, I nodded my understanding, turning towards the backdoor as he threw it open with a seriousness lurking within the depths of his gaze. "Go...now!"

My feet hit the ground running hard as I pushed off from the steps and sprinted directly at the ward I knew would open for me to let me pass. This was a suicide mission because I could see the shadows of men moving from the treeline, their voices carrying with the wind the closer I got. They would see me, there was no way that they couldn't.

Yet, here I was running directly at them.

Tatum's voice echoed in my mind telling me to run, and so that's what I did. The breath in my lungs was cold as I moved across the broken leaves, past the sounds of men, south towards the road.

The farther and farther from the cabin I got, the more silence surrounded me, the darkness of the forest enveloping me. I wasn't sure how far the road was, but after what felt like an eternity running, I knew I was no longer alone. Low growls of wolves resonated somewhere in the forest around me, and my heart beat faster.

The cabin bordered another pack's territory, and it didn't click in my mind when I left that I was going to be running into another pack's territory. One that I wasn't familiar with.

Shit, shit, shit.

Growls grew closer to me as the light at the end of the wooded path came into view. Daylight broke through the branches as the navy blue frame of a car also came into sight, my heart leaping for joy. All I had to do was get there, all I had to do was keep running.

With my mind set on the path ahead, I didn't notice the quickly approaching steps coming near me until a huge force slammed into my side, sending me tumbling through the roots of trees and brush that littered the forest floor. A cry of pain escaped my lips as I palmed the dirt of the ground beneath me. "What the fuck!"

Turning over, I took in the sight of a massive black wolf, its teeth bared at me as it growled in warning. I was used to having dealt with shifters when it came to Logan and his pack, but this creature...it wasn't Logan.

And it wasn't pleased that I was trespassing.

My mind scrambled to find the words needed to speak, but I didn't have to.

Something in the air around us shifted, and the beast before me felt it. The wind began to blow stronger, the leaves on the trees dancing against the shadowed canopies as if screeching at the creature to leave me alone. Fear coursed through me.

A fear I wasn't accustomed to feeling and from somewhere behind me, I felt another presence step forward.

One that made the beast retreat, bowing his head in submission as he took steps back until turning to flee the area. The hairs on the back of my neck stood up as my body went rigid waiting to see what lay behind me. I wanted to look, but I couldn't.

A firm hand on my shoulder made me jump as I looked towards it, catching Tatum's gorgeous eyes. My heart leaped out of my chest as I threw my arms around his neck to hug him after he helped me to my feet. "Oh, thank god."

"I guess I should save you more often." He chuckled, causing me to quickly pull away as I straightened myself.

First the swooning over him kissing me, and now my reaction to him saving me?

I really needed to get laid when this was all over.

"Sorry," I muttered, giving him a small smile as I cast my glance away. "We should probably get going before someone finds us."

He gestured towards the car with his head. "Good idea."

Following him, he removed the branches around the car to help disguise it. The last thing I expected was an old beat up car to be sitting on the side of the road but here it was. Tatum's smile showed nothing but excitement as he unlocked the old beater gesturing for me to climb in.

How in the hell?

My mind raced with how he knew that this was going to happen, and who had been on the phone with him in the kitchen this morning. Things weren't adding up. We climbed into the car, and I couldn't hold back the questions that had been plaguing me.

"Why was the car there?" I muttered as he pulled out onto the highway, his eyes stared straight ahead as he cleared his throat.

"Just in case we needed it."

"So you knew this was going to happen?" I retorted, my gaze watching him as I tried to see how much he was going to tell me or how much he was going to hide.

"No," he replied, clenching his jaw. "But I have a feeling you don't believe that."

A scoff escaped my throat as I shook my head, turning my gaze out the window. "I don't know what I believe, Tatum. You came to me wanting me to trust you. Wanting me to believe you but yet you keep hiding shit."

"Hiding shit...Taylor I've been trying to tell you the truth, and you don't want to believe it."

"Truth?!" I shrieked, "then what the hell was that kiss? Why did it feel like that, and why when I ran, did the hunters not see me?"

His brows furrowed for a moment as his lips parted. "They didn't see you?"

"No, they didn't."

Silence fell over him as he kept his gaze focused ahead. "I don't know what happened when I kissed you. I didn't do or feel anything."

Oh, no. He wasn't going to act like this.

"First a secret holder, and now a fucking liar. Great way to build trust."

CHAPTER TWELVE

Tatum

The last thing I expected was to be running from the hunters myself. I allowed Taylor to escape while I kept the hunters distracted, but they quickly realized what I was up to and in doing so, black-listed me for eternity. Not that I cared much about that, I wasn't planning on staying in this realm for long.

The only problem was it caused conflict for my family. Something my brother wasn't going to be pleased about. Taylor was supposed to be an asset that helped our mission. Instead, she was becoming more of a liability and not one we could afford to get rid of. As much as none of us wanted to admit it, we needed help.

Help that we couldn't get close to home.

To think our safety and survival relied on a woman who didn't even know who she was. Crazy. My parents would never have allowed this, and thinking of them, I could only imagine the lecture I'd end up getting when I returned home. My mother would give me a piece of her mind, but my sister—whose opinion was the only one that mattered—would be proud of me.

Pulling the car out onto the road, Taylor and I sped off, heading out of town and away from the dangers that sought to consume her. Away from her family, who were probably going just as crazy knowing that she was gone, and away from a life I had learned she had built for herself.

She'd be able to start over eventually, finally able to have the peace she so desires. Once my brother and sister were done with her. However, it didn't stop the ache I felt when I watched her look out the car window with a sad expression, as if everything she had worked so hard for had been destroyed in a matter of days.

"I'm sorry about your home."

The comment was meant to comfort her, but she scoffed under her breath and shrugged her shoulders because she didn't want to speak to me. She didn't want to acknowledge I was even there. I just hoped one day she would forgive me because I wished all of this had been easier.

Unsettling silence consumed us as we drove. My mind raced back to her questions and the kiss we had shared. When I kissed her, it wasn't for any particular reason. I did it because it felt right in the moment. The look in her eyes, wide and fearful. Her lip quivering as she sucked in a deep breath trying to calm herself.

It was as if her anxiety had peaked, and I had the urge to make her feel better. An urge to calm and protect her.

The feeling of electricity that flowed through me the moment my lips touched hers was unlike anything I had ever imagined. As if the universe had brought us together for more than just a fleeting moment. As if our destinies were intertwined and our hearts were one.

After that kiss, all that I could think about was her and nothing more. As if she was my world, and nothing outside of her existed.

The heavy conflict of the entire situation weighed heavily on me. How was I supposed to do my job, and bring her back to my sister if I felt the way I did. If every time I was around her I wanted to do sinful things to her?

After stopping at a gas station two hours into Pennsylvania, Taylor settled into the passenger seat like a passenger princess, her shoes off and sunglasses on as the cracked window blew a cool breeze against her skin that danced through her hair. She was beautiful, and the more I tried to ignore that, the harder it was for me to focus on the task ahead.

She was a distraction I welcomed over the last few days and even though I had known her for such a short time. I felt as if I had known her a lifetime.

"Where are we going?" Her words pulled me from my thoughts as I cleared my throat, gripping the steering wheel.

"West. I'll pull over in a few hours so we can rest for the night. It's important we stay ahead of the hunters, though. They are going to be searching for you."

A snort echoed from her. Out of the corner of my eye, she shook her head, slowly turning her gaze towards me. "Well, if we are stuck in a car together for a while, I guess we better continue our conversation from earlier."

"Conversation?"

"Yeah," she snapped, revealing how aggravated she really was. "I mean, what else are we going to do?"

As much as I wanted to enjoy a peaceful moment with her, and thought I was considering her attitude had died down hours ago, it was clear I was sadly mistaken. She had been stewing on whatever it was she wanted to know, and now she thought it was a great time to discuss it.

"Okay then. Why don't you go first?" I didn't blame her for being annoyed about how everything had played out recently, but the constant attitude from her was really getting to me. I wasn't a man who allowed people to speak to me the way she had, and though sometimes I found her comments amusing, I was growing tired of it.

"Why don't you start explaining more about why the hunters want me? I mean, there isn't anything special about me, Tatum. I'm just another supernatural creature."

Of course, she would still think that. The girl was still ignorant to the truth, and though I tried to tell her the truth, I could also understand why she had a hard time believing me. "I already told you why they want you, Taylor."

"Yeah, and that's bullshit—"

"Will you stop!" I finally snapped, tired of her mouth. "If you would actually fucking listen to me for one moment without opening your mouth, you might find that what I have to say makes a lot of fucking sense."

Lips parted and mouth open wide, she stared at me behind dark-rimmed glasses, shocked I had scolded her. But could anyone blame me? She was constantly bitching about everything, and all I was trying to do was help her.

Closing her lips into a tightly met line, she turned her attention back out to the world outside her window. "Fine, I'll listen."

"Will you, though?" I replied sarcastically. "Will you actually listen?"

"Yes," she snapped back, a sneer crossing her lips as she went back to being quiet.

I wasn't sure how much I trusted she would remain quiet because that wasn't who she was. She wasn't the kind of woman to just let things go, at least from what I could tell so far. The moment that I finished putting gas in the car and climbed back in, pulling the car back out onto the highway, I settled in for a conversation I had a feeling wasn't really going to go anywhere.

Taking a deep breath, my eyes scanned the road ahead as I decided how direct to be with her. "I know that you don't want to talk about the Elder Hallow, but we need to. You need to know the truth about it, and who you are before we continue, and you need to try and understand what I'm telling you. It will help you to survive."

"Survive what?" she asked, wariness in her tone.

"Everything that's about to come."

<u>Taylor</u>

The last thing I wanted him to try and discuss with me was the Elder Hallow. I had been raised to cherish it. To trust it, as it was what made us who we are. However, during those lessons, I was also taught that speaking of it to outsiders could destroy everything that we strived so hard to protect. Which was why I was so reluctant to speak on it.

However, there was also a lot I didn't know. Like how they knew about it if it was a secret.

His comment made the hollow pit inside my stomach twist with unease. I didn't understand why I felt the way I did, but perhaps it had a lot to do with how my situation was currently turning out. I mean, a man I barely knew came swooping in with hunters, only to betray them and save me for some...thing they needed.

The rational side of me was yelling like a mad-woman in a movie theater who knew that the main character's best friend was about to die.

"I don't know what to say," I finally responded as I continued to stare out the window in disbelief. "It's hard for me to go against everything I was raised to know."

"I can understand that."

Turning to look at him, I was curious how someone like him, an absolute sex machine on legs, could understand something like that. But I guess we all did have our own secrets and just because he was gorgeous didn't mean he didn't have a past.

"If you understand, then you know it's hard for me to just take your word on things. I get that you are trying to help me, but I don't even understand what you're trying to help me from."

Casting a quick glance at me, he sighed, shrugging his shoulders slightly. "If I tell you what I know, will you promise not to freak out on me and automatically think I'm lying?"

A small snort of laughter escaped me at his question. "Yeah, I can humor you if that's what you want to know."

"Okay..." he muttered, turning off the main highway and onto the interstate. We had been driving for a while, and I still didn't know where we were going besides west. "The Hallow you were told growing up isn't a thing per se. As I said before, you are the Hallow. Your family...as they call themselves, stole you."

"Stole me? That's ridiculous. My mother gave birth to me," I replied quickly. "That much has always been clear."

Again, though, he laughed. "Yeah, she may have helped give birth to your image, Taylor, but she definitely didn't give birth to you. You are far older than you think you are."

That wasn't possible. I had seen my baby pictures growing up. Heard the stories from my family on how I was brought into this world, and that my mother had a difficult time with me. That I was crafted to perfection and the reason why my mother couldn't have any more children. I mean hell, there were hundreds of photos of me as a baby and small child all around the home.

"Not saying that I believe you, but if that's the case, how do you explain the baby photos my mother has?" I asked, expecting him to have no answer but wary when he snorts and his lips meet into a very thin line showing his aggravation.

"They are of you. She took you when you were a child."

There was no way I was going to believe that, and the fact that he was saying this was absurd. Everyone talked of her pregnancy with me. How she couldn't wait to have me.

"It isn't possible. She was pregnant. Everyone knows that."

"Just because she was, doesn't mean that it was with you," he replied, catching me off guard. The implication of his words rendered me momentarily speechless.

My mother was a lot of things, but that extensive of a liar wasn't one of them. No matter how good she thought she was there was no way she would be able to keep a lie up like that. No fucking way she would lie to my sister like that. My sister was her favorite, and if she knew I wasn't her real sister...that girl would have used that bit of information against me a long time ago.

"That's not possible, Tatum," I replied, raising a brow with a smirk on my lips. "Trust me, I know my family."

As much as part of me wanted to believe some of what he was saying, I was having a hard time with it. It just didn't make sense to me her doing something like that and everyone keeping it a secret.

I mean why would they keep it a secret. I'm nobody.

Tired of the conversation, I turned away from Tatum, refusing to look at him. All I wanted to do was get to where we were going fast so I could try and figure out a way to get my life back. If this man really thought I was going to believe my entire life had been some huge elaborate fucking lie...well, he had another thing coming.

CHAPTER THIRTEEN

<u>Taylor</u>

Somewhere, late into the night, Tatum finally decided to pull over so he could sleep. After our conversation, I had remained quiet until I drifted off like the passenger princess I was, only to be awoken by a gentle nudge by Tatum. The blinking light of a Motel 8 wasn't exactly the high end hotel I was hoping for. Not that beggars could be choosers, but finally getting some good sleep didn't sound bad either.

Leaning up against the hood of the car, I watched him make his way back towards me. The dim light of the hotel cast a shadow across his face as my eyes took in the single key in his hand.

Wait...only one key?!

"Where's my room?" I asked casually, hoping he wasn't going to suggest what I thought he was. His eyes lifted to meet mine with a smirk on his lips before he slapped the single key against the palm of his hand.

"Only one room left, unfortunately. But don't worry, there are two beds."

Fuck. That's my damn luck.

"Splendid," I replied with sarcasm, as he gestured for me to follow him.

The more and more time I had to spend with him, the more I was growing used to him being around. But I still didn't trust him. At least, not fully.

I appreciated how he kept me safe and helped me escape the hunters twice. But at the end of the day, it was for his own needs. Just like telling me only bits of information were for his own needs. I could tell one hundred percent that he was hiding shit, and if he didn't think I knew how his mystery caller kept getting us out of a jam, he was sadly mistaken. Yet he avoided explaining anything.

He was in for a rude awakening.

I just needed to do what was best for me and find a way to escape, and once I did, I would take care of myself like I always did.

Slip out into the night. Disappear into the countryside. I'd find a way to stay out of the eyes of the hunters and eventually, they would forget about me.

Or at least that was the hope anyways.

Being a ghost is what I used to be good at, and if I had to do it again, I would. After all, Deidra had always told me to be careful who I trusted. If I felt the need to run then to listen to my gut and do as it was telling me.

I never really understood what she meant that day when she said that, but thinking back on it now, I wonder if she was preparing me for something like this.

As soon as we approached hotel room 208, I regretted being okay with our situation. This hotel wasn't only in the middle of nowhere, but it was also shady as hell. Dim lighting that flickered every now and again, not to mention the random people that seemed to linger on the far side of the walkway. The feeling of their eyes watching me was enough to make the hairs on the back of my neck stand up.

I wasn't one to startle easily, but something about this entire situation didn't sit right with me.

"What's wrong with you?" Tatum's voice broke me out of the daze I was in as I turned my attention from the farside of the walkway back to the door in front of us.

"Uh, nothing," I replied quickly, shrugging my shoulders. "I'm fine. Are you gonna open the door?"

He stared at me, his brow raised before he nodded, opening the door, allowing me to enter the room. The stale smell of cigarette smoke wafted into my nose, causing me to wrinkle it in disgust. The beds looked like they stepped out of a seventies magazine with tacky floral print bedspreads and frills along the bottom. Even the tv was a brown box shape with a silver antenna that showcased just how long it had been since this place had seen some TLC.

"Damn, they could really do with an upgrade," I muttered under my breath as I moved around the room, admiring the rest of the tacky decor before deciding to make the best out of a bad situation.

"Yeah, but it's a place to crash our heads. We will be leaving bright and early anyways."

"Right..." I mumbled as I made my way towards the bed closest to the door. "Well, I guess we better crash."

Laughter resonated through his chest, causing me to stop dead in my tracks. I felt the presence of him slowly creeping behind me. "If you think for one moment that you're taking that bed so you can make the first dash out of here, you're sadly mistaken. You can have the bed near the wall."

Shit. Of course, this prick would think of that. Turning to glance over at him from my shoulder, I narrowed my eyes. "Whatever."

If he wanted to play these games with me, then I was more than happy to play them back with him. Let's see who ends up breaking first, because I can guarantee...it won't be me.

A shove to my shoulder startled me from my sleep, Tatum's voice echoing through my ears. The sluggish feeling of sleep deprivation creeped through my mind as I groaned, rolling over to find Tatum hovering over me. "What the fuck?"

"Get up, we have to go."

I wasn't sure how long I had actually been out, but from the protest in my muscles it hadn't been long enough. Sensing the urgency in his words I quickly sat up, rubbing my eyes with the back of my hand as I glanced around. "What's wrong?"

"There coming. We need to get out of here now."

Shit.

Hearing him say the hunters were coming was enough for me to jump from the bed. I slipped my shoes on and grabbed my sweater. I wasn't sure how long we had, but by the way Tatum quickly grabbed his things and looked at the door, I had a feeling it wasn't long.

"Alright, this is what is going to happen," he said moving towards the window, as he peeked out into the darkened world outside. "The moment I open the door, we are going to rush towards the car. I don't want any arguing from you—"

"There won't be. Can we go now? I don't want to be here when they get here."

Nodding his head, he seemed surprised I was agreeing with him. His hand grabbed the doorknob as he thrusted the door open and we entered back out into the muggy evening air, making our way down the outside corridor straight for the car sitting out in the parking lot.

As much as part of me wanted to ask questions, I didn't.

If keeping my mouth shut and doing what I was told kept the hunters from getting to me, then so be it. As Deidra used to say—it's better the devil you know then the devil you don't.

Climbing into the car with Tatum, he peeled out of the parking lot, leaving the hotel in our rearview mirror. The sight of car lights in the passenger side mirror coming from a distance made my heart throb in my chest as I anticipated a high speed chase. But instead, the lights disappeared into the dimly lit hotel parking lot. A whole five cars, probably loaded with men trying to kill us.

"I don't think they were following us..."

A heavy breath escaped him as he nodded again. "Yeah. I don't think so either. That was close though, way too close."

That was the second time he had known that they were coming before they came. I wasn't exactly sure how he was getting his information, but I was curious.

"Did your mysterious caller text you again about their arrival?"

The question sat heavy in the air between us, and I watched him glance into the rearview mirror before checking his side ones. "Yes, he did."

"Oh, so your mysterious caller is a he?"

"Yes," he muttered again. "It's my brother. You will get to meet him soon."

He was mentioning his family, and I still barely knew anything about him. "How many siblings do you have? If you don't mind me asking."

"I don't think right now is the time for that kind of conversation." Giving him a pointed look he sighed. "You really want to know?"

"Yes, I really want to know."

Glancing at me, a smile crept across the corner of his lips. "I don't mind you asking, Taylor. You're going to meet them all eventually anyways."

"I am?" I replied, not exactly thrilled to be meeting a bunch of new people. I was a loner for the most part.

"Yeah, you are. And to answer your question, I'm one of six."

"Six?!" I gasped. "Jesus, I could never."

Contagious laughter exploded from him, causing me to chuckle to myself. "Sorry, I just...I have never planned on having children."

He was quiet as he shrugged his shoulders. "Never say never. Maybe one day you will change your mind. I mean, you do have all the time in the world, so who knows what you will decide on later down the line."

The thought of having a family of my own actually created an ache in my chest. I had thought about it once upon a time, but I quickly shot the idea down when I realized the kind of world I really lived in. Why would I want to bring a child into a world that was full of hate?

Perhaps the fear was slightly unreasonable to most, but for a supernatural...it was legitimate. People were terrified of what they didn't know, and unfortunately, supernaturals were a minority to the humans who inhabited the earth.

"Maybe if there was a way to live in a society that made it safe enough to raise a child, I would. But this world isn't a place I would want to bring a child into. It's not safe, and I don't believe it ever will be."

I hadn't meant to admit what I did out loud. My words were soft, but I knew that Tatum heard me. He didn't comment like I had expected he would. Instead, he was quiet, as if considering my words carefully.

It wasn't until a few hours into our drive that everything began to spiral. The primal nature of who I was had been deprived for far too long, and because of that, I wasn't able to control the hunger burning inside me. I woke from a short nap in the car to a burning in my chest that took my breath away.

My hand gripped at the center of my chest as a small cry of pain escaped me.

"Taylor?" Tatum questioned, my mind however focused elsewhere. "What's wrong?"

"Nothing!" I snapped, my voice a low growl as the predator instincts within me kicked into high gear. I had to feed. It had been a few days, and usually I would have been okay, but all this sense of panic and running had drained most of the energy I had. My body had burned to the point of non-existence.

"Shit...when was the last time you fed?"

"I'm not hungry—" I snapped at him again, "I'll be fine. Keep driving."

Tatum, however, didn't believe me as he took the next exit towards a public restroom. The dim lights of the parking lot went out as he pulled the car around a darkened area, hiding us from the eyes of humans. Not that there were many around here. A few semi-trucks were parked on the far side of the parking lot. Sleeping truckers unknowing of the danger now lurking near them.

I couldn't feed like this though. If I did, there was a chance I couldn't control myself, and that wasn't something I wanted. The moment the car stopped, I thrust open the door, slamming it behind me. My heart raced as I stumbled towards the bathroom, hoping cold water would help to quench the fire burning across my skin.

"Taylor, wait!" Tatum called out to me as the sound of his footsteps quickly approached. A firm grip to my wrist caused me to turn around with bared teeth as I glared at him.

"I don't want to hurt you."

"Shit. You need to feed, Taylor," he replied with concern in his voice.

Glancing around, I scoffed. "Yeah, I do...okay? I need to fucking feed. But I can't. I can't let these people here get hurt. I'm not like my family, Tatum. This is why I hide. I don't want to hurt anyone, but all this chaos has pushed me to a place of hunger where if I did...I'd kill them."

Ripping my wrist from his grasp, I turned away from him, continuing towards the restroom when his response stopped me dead in my tracks.

"Feed from me."

Slowly, I looked over my shoulder at him. This man was fucking insane. Did he not just hear me say that I would kill someone if I fed like this?

Not that it would be a problem. Killing him would mean that I would be able to get away. No! You can't do that, Taylor. You're not a killer!

The internal battle flowing through me was more than I could handle. I didn't want to be a killer, but standing there watching the shadows dance across his face as he so willingly offered himself up to me was so...tempting.

"You don't know what you're asking for, Ta—"

"I do," he said, stepping towards me. "Take what you need. You can't hurt me."

Before I could answer him, his lips crashed upon mine. The hunger that fueled my soul quickly took over the forefront of my mind. He wrapped an arm around my waist, pulling me close to him. My hand reached up to grip his throat as I inhaled deeply the fresh essence that was this man.

The moment it touched the beast inside me, my body exploded in a way I had never experienced. "What are you?" I whispered, staring at him.

A lazy smile crossed his lips as my hand loosened, giving him opportunity to grasp my hair, pulling my head back as he ran his nose up the length of my throat.

"Someone who is going to fuck you and feed you well into tomorrow, princess."

CHAPTER FOURTEEN

Tatum's lips crashed upon mine. I was lost in a whirlwind of emotions and hunger. Tatum didn't hesitate to pick me up as he carried me to the bathroom. My back quickly pressed against the wall as my mind swirled with the possibilities of what he was offering me. A satisfaction to something inside me that yearned for the life force of anyone else. I wasn't sure what he was, but the taste of him was like nothing I had ever experienced before.

Our movements were rough and aggressive as I pulled at his shirt. The sound of material tearing under my touch as I fed on him little by little echoed throughout the bathroom. One hand pulled at my pants as his other aimed for my throbbing core. My mind drifted to the fact we could be caught at any moment, but my hunger was enough to make me not care about the situation at all.

"I want you," I whispered as his fingers slipped beneath the top of my pants, down across my mound, and straight into my aching center. A moan slipped from my lips as his finger stretched me. I may have been a succubus, but I didn't fuck everyone I fed from. It had been a long time since I fed properly and let a man take me. Sex during feeding was an intimate moment, and where most succubus fed like that all the time, I did not.

"God, you're so wet, aren't you?" He growled, thrusting his fingers up roughly, causing me to moan again. "You like that, don't you?"

"Yes," I gasped, nodding my head. "Stop teasing me and fuck me already."

"You will get what I'm giving you."

I wasn't sure what he meant by that, but I had a feeling I was going to find out.

Tatum kissed his lips over my jaw. His fingers worked themselves inside me as his free hand trailed gently down my skin until they were at the top of my pants. The ache he created when his hand left caused me to whimper. He pulled my pants down to my knees. Confusion swirled in my mind as I tried to understand why he stopped, only to be replaced with surprise as he dropped to his knees. His mouth latched onto my core with a hunger I hadn't expected.

"Fuck!" I cried out as his tongue swirled around my throbbing clit. My mind raced as he thrusted his fingers inside me one more, the dual sensation driving me mad.

For the first time in my life, I wasn't in control of my situation. The hunger in me was better than it was only thirty minutes before, but the desire to have him fuck me senseless was higher than it had been when we came in here.

I wanted him...fuck, I needed him, and he had no idea how much.

My body called to him as if begging for him to nourish it. As if the very essence of his being was the only thing that could sustain who I was. My entire body was on fire from his touch as my pores seemed to soak in every ounce of him. I didn't understand how it was that my powers didn't seem to affect him. How lively he was after me draining him, how in control he still was after everything.

The sound of people out in the parking lot caused my eyes to go wide as I fisted Tatum's hair, trying to stop him. "Someone's coming."

His only response was a low growl as his movements became faster. Air left my lungs as he pinned me to the wall, my legs spread but restricted by my jeans as he continued to fuck me in a way I couldn't resist.

There was no stopping him, and the fact someone was about to walk in the bathroom only made my heart race faster as my stomach knotted with the impending pleasure about to wash over my body.

The footsteps were on the concrete outside. Tatum shoved my wrist into my mouth, biting down as a scream ripped from my throat. A surge of pleasure rushed through my body as my eyes rolled into the back of my head, unable to contain the pleasure he had created in me.

It wasn't until he lapped every bit of my orgasm did, he finally rise to his feet once more. His hands pulled up my pants as he buttoned them back in place, fixing my shirt as he let me lean against him.

"What the fuck was that?" I asked breathlessly. Trying to understand how he could fuck me with his mouth like that, feed me, and expect nothing in return.

However, instead of giving me a reply, he smiled and turned towards the door.

"Come on, we still have a long drive ahead of us."

Tatum

Rule one. Never get involved with your contact.
Well, I fucking broke that shit.
Did every part of me want to fuck the shit out of her in that bathroom? Absolutely.

Was I going to let that happen? No fucking chance.

As much as every part of my body wanted me to ravage Taylor like she was my last meal, I couldn't. I had a job to do, and what I did for her back there at that rest area was simply to help her with her hunger. She was in need and as her caretaker until I got her back to my home, I had to do what was necessary to make sure she was comfortable.

Yeah, that's what I was going with.

The sight of her head tilted back as her eyes rolled, and her lips parted was something that would be forever imprinted in my mind. I felt her body pulling at my soul, taking what she needed until she was satisfied. I had seen what she did with the shifter, a task that was thankfully interrupted before she had killed it.

But tonight, I experienced her power firsthand.

The only problem was it wasn't the power of a succubus. Even though that's what she thought she was.

Taylor slept peacefully in the passenger seat next to me as I contemplated everything going to happen next. Arriving in my hometown at the house I grew up in wasn't what I had expected. But unfortunately, those were the cards I had been dealt.

My brother had informed me how hard it was going to be to accomplish this mission, but I didn't have another choice. She was an asset to my queen. A ruler in her own right, and I had to ensure her safety above everything else.

I just hadn't expected to feel the way I did about her. I hadn't expected for her to come into my life and completely turn shit upside down. Yeah, she didn't push me to the brink of death while she was feeding on me, due to my special circumstances. Not that she knew that. But also, because something else was between us.

I couldn't help but feel my connection with her was deeper. Like a familiar soul I had met once upon a time. An echo of my own heart, though it didn't exactly beat anymore.

Everything about this woman drove me absolutely insane, and in a good way.

My mind constantly wandered to images of her naked beneath me. Her back arched and perky tits pressed against my chest as she stared at me with those big doe eyes, begging for pleasure I so desperately wanted to give her.

It took everything in me not to fuck her own the spot, and now I was left with a throbbing cock that would decide when it wanted to come and go for the past few hours we had been driving. The torment at not being able to have her to sate my own lust was nerve wracking.

But I knew my place.

In the end, she would have to accomplish her destiny, and she would have no place with me. There was no point in possibly starting something if I knew we both couldn't have it.

It wouldn't have been fair to her in the long run.

Casting my eyes back to her sleeping form, I couldn't help but take in every single detail. Her hair cascaded in soft waves around her face and over her shoulders. Thick black lashes laid gently against her cheeks. The rise and fall of her chest as she slept.

She was beautiful...breathtaking even.

My phone buzzed in my pocket, pulling me from thoughts of Taylor. As much as I didn't feel like talking to anyone right now, I already knew who it was before I answered. There was only one person who would be calling me, and that was my brother.

"Hello?" I said, as I placed the phone to my ear trying to keep my voice low.

"Where are you?" my brother asked for the millionth time since we had left her cabin.

"About thirty minutes out. I've been driving straight through since the incident at the hotel."

A deep chuckle reverberated through the phone. "Yeah, I figured that. You left that damn hotel last night. I had figured you would have been here by now."

I drove straight through the night and after a day and a half, I was close to my destination. It wasn't like Idaho was a quick drive from the border of Indiana. Shit took time, and we had to make stops to eat and fill the car back up. Though, he wouldn't understand that. Everything to him was taking too much time.

"I'll be pulling up shortly. I'm almost to the main road now," I replied, trying to keep the conversation short. The last thing I wanted was for Taylor to hear too much. Until she was behind safe gates, I didn't want to risk her changing her mind and running.

"Alright. I'll alert the pack to your arrival."

Hanging up the call, I pushed my phone back into my pocket. I was glad Taylor was familiar with shifters due to the nature of my family, but I had a feeling when things started to play out here, she wasn't going to take kindly to the way my brother handled things.

He had never been graceful with information, and Taylor wasn't exactly easy to explain shit to.

I turned on the main road that led into pack lands, the wave of my brother's authority radiating around me. It was like a soft buzz within the air that would have told me who to obey, but I was no longer under his rule. However, Taylor began to stir, and I wondered if she could feel it too.

"Where are we?" she groaned, slowly sitting up. Her arms stretched around her as she moved up into the seat, her eyes scanning the thick tree lines around us. A soft golden glow shone around her, her powers charged for now and a happiness seeming to fall over her. My gifts, the only thing that let me know she was okay. "Tatum...where are we?"

"My family home," I replied with a heavy breath. "We will be safe here."

She was quiet as the car pulled down one gravel road after another until the tall white and black structure of the pack house came into view. There were many different buildings that lingered nearby. Most of which belonged to pack members, but even a library lingered...my mother's pride and joy.

"How sure are you about that safety situation?"

Confused by her question, I wrinkled my brow, pulling the car to a stop and parking. "Pretty sure. No one here will harm you, Taylor. I promise."

Stepping from the car, Taylor followed but with extreme caution. Something I found sweet and amusing at the same time. The lights were still on as the front door opened, showing the shadowed figure of my brother, a man I hadn't seen in years.

Seeing him again brought a smile to my face. I stepped forward, his arms open wide as he embraced me into a hug. "Aww, little brother, it's so good to see you again. Phone calls do us no justice."

"I know the feeling," I replied with a smile. "This, brother, is Taylor."

My words fell short as I turned to Taylor, watching as her once confused expression turned into that of a sneer as she let her eyes dart between my brother and I.

"You've got to be fucking kidding me," she snapped with irritation. "Pollux, the Gemini twin, is your fucking brother?"

Fuck...they knew each other?! What the fuck didn't he tell me now?

CHAPTER FIFTEEN

<u>Taylor</u>

A million emotions ran through me when I laid eyes on Pollux. The most threatening one being anger. It coursed through me like a raging river, consuming every inch of my sanity as I stared at him with a hatred I hadn't felt in so long. Sure, it had been thirty years since I had seen the man and age had not been kind to him. However, his face—his eyes—were something I would never forget.

"Hello again, my lady."

My lady? Was he fucking kidding me right now?

His words were meant to be respectful, but I took them with a sour taste in my mouth. He had called me that the first time I met him. The first time he came to visit Deidra, and she shushed him away, telling me to remain inside while she handled the Alpha, who was too greedy for his own good.

I hadn't known what it meant back then, but when she died, I realized his greed must have been what killed her. Had he left us alone, she might still be alive.

"You have *some* fucking nerve showing your face to me again," I sneered before my eyes turned to Tatum. "And you...you were part of *this*?"

Tatum stared at me with his lips parted and a furrowed, confused look upon his face as he turned to his brother. "Am I missing something?"

Ah, so it seems dirty little secrets are Pollux's specialty.

Curiosity filled me as I crossed my arms over my chest, waiting to see if Pollux was going to tell his brother what he obviously hadn't been privy to know before. Yet, Pollux remained quiet before turning back towards the house, slowly walking away.

"Let's get inside. There is a lot to discuss."

"Is he being serious right now?" I gasped with annoyance.

Tatum turned to me with a heavy breath and shrugged his shoulders. "I don't know, honestly. Let's just go inside and talk there."

"Absolutely not." There was no way in hell I was going into that house. For all I knew, I'd never be allowed to leave again. Pollux was responsible for Deidra's death. That was the only thing I was sure of, and I had sworn so long ago I would make him pay for what he did to her—what he did to me.

"Taylor," he sighed, shaking his head. "Please don't make this difficult."

"Difficult?!" I all but yelled in shock at his statement. "You have no idea—"

"Stop." He quickly shut me down. "You're right...I don't have any idea what the hell has happened between you and my brother. But what I *do* know is that this is the safest place we can be when it comes to running from the hunters. So please, come inside."

Every part of me wanted to be stubborn, but I knew I couldn't leave. We had barely escaped the hunters when we left the hotel, and I had no doubt they were surely on their way here. But if Tatum's family was the most renowned pack I had thought them to be, the hunters wouldn't be stupid enough to storm this place.

"Fine," I seethed with a huff, rolling my eyes as I made my way towards the house, passing Tatum, who let out a chuckle as he followed behind me.

I entered the house and was taken aback by the outdated display of decor. Floral wallpapers and warm-colored walls with white trim. All of which were accented with bronze colored decor that were elements of the woman of the house, no doubt.

However, as I looked around at the many accents, I also noted the dust collected on top of tables and picture frames. Something no royal woman would allow to happen in her home. Which made me wonder where Pollux's mate was because it wasn't like a woman of the home to not greet her guests.

"Where is everyone?" I muttered as Tatum came to stand by my side.

"Long gone," he replied, causing my gaze to turn to him before he turned and disappeared further down the hall and through a doorway light danced upon.

I wasn't sure what he meant by 'long gone', but I wanted to know. If I was going to figure out what these men wanted from me, and how I was going to seek my revenge, it was best I find out everything there was to find out. One of those, keep your friends close and your enemies closer.

Taking a deep breath, I pressed forward into the room Tatum had disappeared in. The only light within the room was a blazing fire in the fireplace, casting shadows upon the piles of books and papers that lay scattered around.

I had never seen such a disarray, something so chaotic. Especially coming from one of the largest packs in North America.

"Did your housekeeper quit?" I muttered, Pollux not acknowledging me as Tatum seemed to groan at my comment. A single side glance from him caused me to shrug my shoulders as I rolled my eyes.

Moving slowly about the room, my eyes fell upon Pollux, seated behind the dark wooden desk. His gaze set upon me with his hands clasped, as if watching my movements were the most entertaining thing he had seen in a while.

"Please, take a seat. So we can begin."

"Begin? That's saying it politely," I retorted, taking a seat in one of the brown chairs in front of his desk. Tatum chose to remain standing behind the other, as if waiting for something to happen. Which made me even more uncomfortable than I was.

"I know that you don't like me, and I have a feeling why. But I want you to know that I didn't hurt your friend Taylor."

"Don't lie to me," I snapped, the memories trying to resurface but my strong-willed mind refusing them access. "I know what I saw, Pollux."

He paused as if controlling his next words before lifting a glass filled with amber liquid to his lips. "No, you know what you think you saw, Taylor."

What I thought I saw? "What the hell does that mean?"

"It means that there is much that you need to know, Taylor. A lot was kept from you, like these..." Pollux reached into a brown box upon his desk, and pulled out a bundle of parchment tied with twine, setting them upon the desk in front of me.

I didn't have the slightest clue what was in them, but I could tell straight away that they were letters. But I didn't understand why he was giving them to me.

Reaching forward, I gently lifted the stack of letters and pulled them towards me. My hands fiddled over them as I took in the writing on the front letter on top. My heart lurched forward, instantly recognizing the handwriting.

"These are from Deidra?" I gasped, my eyes lifted to meet his.

"They are, and before you jump to conclusions…I think you need to read what those contain. It will help you to understand what has been going on for many years, Taylor."

Unsure of what to think or what to believe, I sat in stunned silence. My eyes fell again to the letters as I attempted to comprehend what he was saying. Deidra had been writing letters to him, letters that contained information that pertained to me…or about my situation.

I wasn't sure, but as Deidra's last words to me rolled through my mind, I knew the only way I was going to find the truth about anything was to do as Pollux suggested. Read the letters and have faith that eventually everything would be clear.

"Deidra…" I whispered. "You have no idea how much I need you right now."

I needed her, and though I knew she wasn't around to guide me anymore, her words always lingered in my mind. *I will always be with you, Taylor.*

CHAPTER SIXTEEN

<u>Tatum</u>

I hadn't expected when we arrived that my brother would take it upon himself to divulge information to Taylor he hadn't even shared with me. Information that could have been crucial to finding her to begin with. Watching him hand a bundle of letters to Taylor as if he had been waiting a lifetime to give them to her made me angry.

"I will have someone show you to a room," Pollux said after a moment of silence. "You both have had a long trip, and I'm sure you would like time to yourself to get cleaned up and enjoy an evening of rest."

Taylor didn't say anything. She simply nodded her head and stood to her feet as one of the few servants left in the home entered without saying a word to guide her to her room. I wasn't sure what was going through her head, but something about the look on her face made me want to comfort her.

My little time with her the past few days had taught me that though she had been through a ton of shit in her life, she still cared about everything. Which was strange to me considering those I had met of her kind before didn't really care about anyone but themselves.

Succubi were known for being selfish creatures who only cared about their next fix.

But Taylor was different.

She left, and I turned my attention to my brother, trying to keep my temper together as I went over everything that had recently happened. "Why does she know you?"

My gaze met his, and I saw the look of defeat within his eyes I had only seen once before when Trixie and his daughter left for the Fae realm. She had begged him to go with her, but they both knew it wasn't his time.

"Remember the day mom died?"

His question wasn't one I was expecting, but I remembered the day well. It was the same day Silas recruited me for my current task.

"Yeah, of course I do," I replied, running my hand through my hair as I walked around to take a seat across from him. "I don't think any of us who were there can forget that day. It's permanently engraved in my mind."

Pollux nodded in understanding, lifting his cup and draining the rest of its contents. "We were there for her."

"For Taylor?"

"Yep, for Taylor," he replied calmly. "I had been trying for weeks to convince Deidra, Taylor's mentor, that we could keep Taylor safe. That the humans had found out what she was and that her own family were lying to her."

"Yeah, her family kidnapped her. I tried to explain that to her, but she didn't believe me."

Pollux's gaze turned into a narrowed, angry expression. I wasn't supposed to have told her that, but it felt like the right thing to do, so I went against protocol. "That wasn't your place, Tate."

Shrugging my shoulders, I brushed off his comment. "Yeah, well, I did. It felt right in the moment and I don't understand why everything has to be so secretive in this family, brother. I'm tired of it, aren't you?"

"It isn't that the secrets are on purpose, Tate. You will learn that once you grow up a bit more."

"Don't talk to me like a child," I sneered, rolling my eyes.

"Then stop acting like one!" he roared, slamming his hand down upon the desk. "I can't afford for you to fuck this up, damn it."

I had seen my brother angry many times, but I didn't understand why he was angry now. I did what I was supposed to. I had brought her here, and eventually, I would be taking her back to Asgard for Cassie. The fact that he was pissed off was ridiculous, and I was done with it.

"Don't fucking raise your voice to me, brother. I'm not the same kid you once knew, and you damn well know that. This place..." I replied, gesturing to his home, "is only a halfway point to where we are really going. That is all it was ever meant for."

"Are you insinuating something?"

A scoff escaped me as I let the corner of my lips turn up into a partial smile. "Take it however you want, *brother.*"

His lips met together in a fine line, staring at me with the same hatred he had thirty-years ago. He hadn't wanted me to be part of this back then, and he damn sure didn't want me part of it now. All he ever said was that I was a liability. A constant reminder of our sister and her rule over him and everything he claimed to be his.

That wasn't the truth.

Pollux had never gotten over what happened between him and my sister so many years ago. I was only a teenager back then, but it changed something in him nonetheless. When Trixie left, it was like she took the last bit of his humanity with her to the Fae realm.

But that's why we were here, for Pandora.

My brother's daughter, an heir in her own right. A power player, a child born to celestial magic before my brother had given his powers to Cassie to restore her immortal life. Powers that the child couldn't control, the same as Cassie's daughter Faeryn. Something about the female bloodline unable to contain the gifts they were given at birth.

"Don't think that you're special just because you're bringing her back. It will change nothing for your future placement in Cassie's empire."

"Cassie's empire—" I gasped, laughter escaping me as I shook my head. "She is our fucking queen, Pollux. She has saved our asses more than once, and with our grandfather off dealing with other shit, she is the one we answer to."

My brother wanted to open his mouth to say something else, but quickly decided against it the moment I raised my brow, curious to know what he was going to say.

"I can see this conversation is going nowhere," he finally replied, changing the subject. "I believe it's best we both retire tonight. Then we can pick up our conversation in the morning when we are both more level-headed."

A snort escaped me as I smiled, nodding. "Sure. I'll stay where I always do."

Climbing to my feet, I didn't bother to address Pollux again as I made my way from his office towards the stairs. I didn't need someone to show me around. I had spent enough time in this house to know exactly where I needed to go. Even if it had been years since Pollux and I had been reacquainted with one another.

Taking the stairs two and a time, I was ready to shower and call it a night. It would probably take hours for me to actually fall asleep, but a quiet place to think was what I was more interested in.

That, and the fact I needed to contact Silas.

My eyes scoured the various photos that littered the walls. Happy photos of Trixie, Pollux, and their children were everywhere. However, dust from years of not being tended gave them a faded feeling that made me wonder if Pollux had even stepped foot up here in quite some time.

It wasn't news to anyone that he had spent countless nights after they departed in the downstairs guest room, refusing to sleep in a bed that his wife once laid in. The heartbreak he suffered after she left took such a toll he didn't want to be here at all. The only reason why he was here was because his son—Malachi—was the heir who would take over his throne.

The bastard heir Pollux swore would never see the chance to rule, hence why he has continued to refuse his son the pack. Not that I really could understand why. The kid wasn't a bad kid, just angry and misunderstood.

The closer I got to my room, the louder sounds of crying became apparent until I was stopped outside the door across from where I would be staying, listening to Taylor on the other side.

I wasn't sure what she was going through, nor could I fathom what was in those letters, but I wanted to comfort her. An urge I didn't understand considering I shouldn't have felt anything for her at all.

Since I met her, I had been enraptured with her. My desire to please her, be with her, was something I couldn't control. It was as if every part of me felt connected to her on a level that shouldn't have been possible.

Taking a deep breath, I laid my hand upon her door, my forehead touching the cool white wood as I closed my eyes, listening to her gentle sobs. I hated that she was in pain, but all I could hope was that whatever was in the letters my brother gave her was the closure she needed to move on.

Or the answers she needed to be who Silas said she was meant to be.

"Taylor," I whispered, not wanting to bother her but needing to know she was okay.

"Go away, Tatum."

"Look, I'm sorry that this all happened. Are you okay?" I asked, knowing full well the question was ridiculous because how could she be okay at a time like this?

She was silent before sounds of footsteps made their way towards the door, causing me to step back quickly as it opened. Her big blue eyes stared up at me with irritation, red and puffy from all the crying she must have done.

"Did you seriously ask me if I was okay?"

Opening and closing my mouth, I sighed before nodding. "Yeah, I guess I did."

"Why?"

"Why what?" I replied.

"Why do you care if I'm okay? I mean, you brought me here. Since the moment I met you, shit has gone fucking batshit crazy, and now I find out that you were part of the group that killed the woman I cared for...all for a power that I don't have."

A power she doesn't have. If she only knew the truth.

There was no way that I was going to even contemplate diving into that conversation right now. She was too distraught and needed time to process everything. Opening my mouth would only make things worse in the long run.

"I'm sorry for bothering you. I'll let you get some rest." Giving in was the only thing I knew to do, and turning from her, I opened the bedroom door behind me and disappeared from her sight, into the dark cold void I called home for a long time.

Perhaps she wasn't the only one who needed to gain some closure. It seemed like we all needed it lately, including my brother, who was undoubtedly sulking downstairs in his office still.

Reaching for the light, I flipped the switch, letting the yellow fluorescents light the room to a dull yellow glow. Everything was the same as I had left it. Blue blankets trimmed in black, old posters on the walls, and the same dust on the dresser that littered the rest of the house.

"Nice," I muttered sarcastically to myself as I listened to Taylor's door closing.

If I was going to get her back to Asgard in any kind of form, I really had to find a new game plan because this woman was going to be the death of me if I did not.

CHAPTER SEVENTEEN

<u>Taylor</u>

As soon as Tatum closed his bedroom door, I crumbled. I hadn't even opened the letters Pollux had given me yet, but the thought of her writing to him—of her keeping secrets from me—it killed me. I didn't want to remember her for such things. I wanted to remember her for the woman I knew, not the woman she may have really been.

"Get a hold of yourself," I groaned.

I had kept myself together for years, and here I was an emotional mess like a fucking teenager who didn't know how to deal with life. It was pathetic, and I felt pathetic. A fucking succubus who was over emotional. What an ironic concept to think about.

I didn't want the memories I cherished with her to be tainted by the possible lies that she kept. Confliction weighed heavily on me, and I knew I was going to have to face the possibilities of what the letters did hold.

A truth that could set me free from a life of confusion.

Or maybe there were just things Pollux constructed to get me to trust him.

Wiping the tears from my cheeks, I sat on the queen size bed in the middle of the room. The black swirling damask blankets stood out against the white walls, the letters upon it a highlighted focal point that clearly didn't belong.

This place wasn't as bad as I had expected it to be, and no matter how unwilling I had been to come here, I felt safe. In a strange kind of way.

Maybe I'm developing Stockholm syndrome...

Slowly, I gathered the courage I needed until the letters were once again in my hand, my fingers pulling at the twine until I could freely sift through them.

Twenty-eight. There were twenty-eight letters sent between her and Pollux over some crazy extended period of time, and I never noticed.

How in the hell did I never notice?

"Please don't let me hate you, Deidra," I whispered, pleading with the gods to give me at least that much. She had been a rock-like figure for me for as long as I could remember and finding out it was all bullshit wasn't something I wanted to go through.

Fiddling with the first letter, I pulled the parchment from its envelope while holding back tears that threatened to fall as I took in Deidra's handwriting.

Dearest Lux,

Thank you for reaching out to me about the guardian. I can't confirm her whereabouts, but what I can say is my sources tell me she is safe. They also tell me she isn't aware of what she is, and I don't believe she is involved with the Hallow. The girl, from what I have been told, is very naive to the ways of our world, but I still don't know enough about her to share information.

Please give me time, and I will see what I can find out.

Deidra

Guardian? What the hell was a guardian?

I didn't have the slightest clue what guardian she was talking about, and from the sounds of it she hadn't even met me at this point. Or that was how she was making it out. Knowing Deidra, she was lying. One thing she used to always tell me was that I was safe with her. That if I had to become invisible, she could make me invisible.

I never saw it as a threat. Instead, it was a warm, safe feeling that the words created and every part of what she told me I trusted.

Laying the letter down, I pulled out another. I wasn't quite sure how many of these I really wanted to go through but nothing was going to make any sense until I attempted to understand. Taking a look at the date, I frowned. The date was a few months after the first letter, and the writing was much longer than the first.

Dearest Lux,

I'm sorry to hear about your daughter. I know you and your wife are doing everything you can to help her, but as I told you when I saw you months ago, I can't help her. I understand your frustration, but I will remind you that things aren't always what we want them to be.

As I said back then, it's best she return to her people. Your wife has already felt the effects of being in this realm for years, and it isn't going to get better until she leaves. I, myself, don't have a mate like shifters do, but I understand how hard it is to consider letting someone you love go.

The guardian isn't the answer to what you are seeking. She has been through a lot, and the last thing she needs is to be hassled when she doesn't even seem to know of her role or her past. The people who took her did something. Every part of who she was has been wiped, and because of that, I have no idea where the Hallow is.

I need to read more of my mother's journals to understand.

I need more time.

She can't tell us anything if she doesn't know who she is. I have spent time with her, but even in that short amount of time, I can say without a doubt she knows nothing about any of it. Perhaps

Moria took the Hallow when the guardian was taken. I will keep you posted if I find anything else.
    Deidra

My brows furrowed in confusion, hearing about Pollux's daughter. It was clear there was something serious going on with her, and the way Deidra spoke about his wife not being from this realm puzzled me. If she wasn't from here, then what the hell was she?

Growing up, my nanny used to tell me stories of other realms. However, I had always considered them to be just what she said, fairy tales. Of course, supernaturals themselves were considered fairytales, but that wasn't the same. We all resided on Earth, the only realm that was real. Wasn't it?

Taking a moment to think about what she said, I read over my mother's name again. 'Perhaps, Moria took the Hallow...' What did that even mean? The Hallow was our source of power. It wasn't an object, it was a place. An entity of its own right. Yet, everywhere I turned, people had their own assumptions of what it could be.

Flipping the envelope over, I took in the date again, and scoffed with a smile. Deidra had lied to Pollux. I had been residing with her when she wrote this. Which means he hadn't been to her home. At least that was what I would assume.

Thinking back, I tried to remember details of this time period. Anything I could that would help give me clarity to what we had been doing at this time, but I couldn't. I remembered a lot of things, but there were still times when my memory wasn't as good as it could have been.

But that could have been from the amount of partying I did back then with Logan and his pack. Damn wolves knew how to throw a good party for sure.

Still, knowing that Deidra referenced my mother the way she did made me more curious about what Tatum had said. I had never felt close to her, but she was the mother I knew my entire life. Or so I thought.

With Deidra not around anymore, there wasn't a way for me to ask her these questions and that killed me. I needed to speak to her, needed her guidance more than anything.

Letter after letter, I read through everything that Deidra had said to Pollux. By the time I got to the last one, I felt shattered and completely exhausted. My mind, thoroughly done with everything.

How was it that Deidra and the others were able to keep something like this from me for so long?

Laying back upon the bed, I let the parchment fall from my hand to the floor, my eyes staring at the textured ceiling above me as if it was the most interesting thing in the room. "Fuck my life," I whispered.

If I was going to gain any clarity about anything, I was going to have to suck it up and listen to what Pollux had to say. As much as I didn't want to, there had to have been a reason for everything, and figuring out that reason needed to be at the top of my list no matter how much I hated him.

His face was the last thing I saw the night she was killed. His face was the image that hovered over her dead body as I hid in the treelines, trying to keep out of sight. I had lost myself that night at the cabin, and even with the powers I had, it wasn't enough to save her.

Trying to stay awake, I ran my hand down over my face in an attempt to keep myself focused. But the harder I tried, the more the desire to sleep crept in. My mind clouded over in a distant fog before I finally succumbed to the darkness that begged me to join it.

Waking the next morning, I found myself twisted within the blankets. An ache throbbed in my head as I groaned and patted my hand upon the mattress in search of my phone. I wasn't sure what time it was or how long I had been asleep, but the need to use the bathroom and brush my teeth was an urgency I had to attend to.

Slowly I rolled over, the crunching of paper echoing around me as I dragged myself towards the bathroom. The white marble and glass shower greeted me when I turned the light on, shielding my eyes from the brightness.

"Jesus Christ," I grumbled as I stared at my reflection in the mirror. "You look like shit."

It wasn't even twenty-minutes later that banging on the bathroom door caused me to all but jump out of my skin. Turning off the hot water, I snatched the towel off the wall hanger, my eyes wide as my heart raced.

"Who is it?!"

"Look, I know you're pissed about being here, but do you really have to use all the fucking hot water in the house?" The voice belonged to Pollux, and the fact he was banging on my door acting like that as his age pissed me off.

Wrapping the towel around my body, I climbed out of the shower and threw the door open to face him. "Are you being serious right now? Get the fuck out of my room, you weirdo. I'm sure your WIFE wouldn't approve of you storming in here!"

Pollux's angry expression quickly turned to one of shock as he stared at me, standing before him in my partially concealed dripping wet glory. "What did you just say?"

"You heard what I said, Pollux. I get this is your house and all, but I didn't ask to be here. So why don't you fucking leave instead of staring at me while I'm in nothing but a towel."

Teasing and seductive me wouldn't have minded it if it had been Tatum standing before me instead of Pollux. Hell, normal me would have willingly dropped the towel had bent over the bed allowing Tatum to ravish me.

But Pollux was like a bucket of cold water to anyone's primal sexual urge.

Pollux didn't bother to argue with me as I watched him take two steps back and turn, leaving. My eyes quickly connected with Tatum, who stood shirtless with black sweatpants hanging low off his hips.

Sweet goddess, it's like the universe heard my pleas.

Memories of what happened between us back at the rest stop instantly flooded my mind. As much as I could pretend, I didn't care, it was hard to keep my composure around him. Especially when my eyes kept drifting to the south of his waistband.

"Taylor, did you hear me?"

His words snapped me out of my daze, a slow heat crawled across my cheeks, and I realized I had been caught daydreaming of things I shouldn't have been.

"I'm sorry, what did you say?" I asked, clearing my throat trying to avoid eye contact.

"I said that there should be some of my sister's old clothes in that closet that will fit you. Are you okay?"

Again, the heat in my cheeks deepened. He was over here trying to help me get clothes, and I'm standing like a fool admiring the package between his thighs. If the universe was able to open up right now and swallow me whole, I'd appreciate it.

"Oh," I gasped, finally looking at him with a smile. "Thanks. I'll check that out."

He nodded, raising a brow with curiosity. "Okay, I'll see you downstairs then."

Reaching into the room, he grabbed the doorknob, shutting the door behind him. Once the door was closed, I slumped onto the bed with a groan. "What the fuck is wrong with me?"

I had tasks to stay on top of. Questions that needed answers.

I couldn't allow myself to get lost in the bullshit with him!

Even if sex with him was at the forefront of my mind right now.

CHAPTER EIGHTEEN

<u>**Taylor**</u>

By the time I got dressed and found the courage to head downstairs, I was an emotional mess. I was trying to find something presentable with the clothes his sister had abandoned, but I couldn't stop thinking of Tatum. Never in my life had anyone ever gotten me as flustered as he had.

I felt like a hormonal teenager eager to get herself off at the first man willing to take a second look at her, and it was incredibly disturbing. How was I supposed to stay focused if the smell of him made my thighs press together with anticipation.

Get yourself together. What the fuck is wrong with you?!

The constant mental reprimands were a little much, but it was the only thing I knew to do to keep myself sane in the moment.

Maybe it was from when I fed off him.

Maybe whatever he was made me this way.

Stopping at the bottom of the stairs, I took a deep breath, running my fingers through my hair before moving down the hall where I assumed was the kitchen. Pollux and Tatum's voices were low, but I had heard my name as clear as day, causing me to stop before I turned the corner.

"...we need her to cooperate..."

"Yes, and that's why I have asked for help with this situation. It's clear that you won't be able to help me prepare her for Asgard on your own. She can't stand to be around you."

Tatum's words were pretty on point. I couldn't stand Pollux. He was a complete asshole. Had he tried to be nice when I first got here? Yes. But I also knew that him being nice was fake as fuck. He was only acting this way because he wanted something.

And that doesn't really make for a desirable circumstance of trust building.

"What are you talking about?" Pollux said quickly, as if he was hesitant and unsure about what Tatum said about bringing someone else in to help me.

"You heard what I said, Pollux. This is out of your league and I don't want to have to referee whatever is going on between you two," Tatum replied with an exhausted sort of sigh. The sound of a chair sliding across the floor caught my attention. "Who did you call, Tate?"

Laughter escaped Tatum as he replied, "You'll see."

"I don't—"

Realizing that the conversation was getting far more heated than it probably needed to be, I decided to make my presence known. Before, things got way out of hand.

Stepping forward, I turned the corner with a new sense of determination as I entered the kitchen. "Good Morning."

Their eyes connected with mine as their conversation died. Pollux's mouth quickly snapped shut before turning back towards the stove, where it seemed he had been busy cooking. If tension could kill, I'd have been dead the moment I stepped foot into the kitchen where they were.

"Did you sleep well?" Tatum asked with a straight face.

"Uh, yeah, I guess," I replied, trying to act as I hadn't been eavesdropping. "I am starving, though."

His brows raised slightly, and his smile widened. I, of course, was talking about food, but the route in which my mind seemed to travel definitely wouldn't have had me saying no. Even if I was trying to pretend that I didn't want him to ravish me.

"Well, there is plenty, so help yourself," Pollux called out. His voice interrupted the silent moment I was having with Tatum, causing me to break my gaze and turn towards the table, admiring the spread he had created.

"Looks delicious."

"Yeah, Pollux has always liked to cook," Tatum piped up as he gestured for me to take a seat, which I gladly accepted on the far opposite side of the table from him. If I was going to make it through the day, I was going to have to keep my distance from him.

The closer I was to him, the more of a distraction he became.

The men began to speak casually to each other, talking about how things were going within the pack since Tatum had last been there. I wasn't sure if it was because they wanted me to eat before discussing things with me, but I wasn't going to oppose a moment of nourishment before having to get down to business.

I took a deep breath, lifting my glass to my lips as I tried to focus my attention on the conversation at hand. I didn't want to seem rude, and settled for acting like I was paying attention. But even with the space between Tatum and I, it was hard.

There was something about the way he looked at me, the way his eyes lingered on my face, that ignited a spark within me; a spark I desperately wanted to extinguish.

Stay focused. He is only doing his job. Don't let yourself get carried away.

No matter how much I tried to internally reprimand myself, I couldn't help but allow those thoughts to silence within my mind as the lust-filled control pushed forward. Shifting uncomfortably in my seat, I tried to find a distraction in the rather large kitchen area. The aroma of freshly brewed coffee filled the air, and the sound of the chime on the oven letting Pollux know that the baked goods were done.

I needed anything to divert my attention from the thoughts that threatened to consume me. It was like a magnetic force, pulling me towards him despite my best efforts to resist. I had gone to bed last night overwhelmed with the letters, and now this morning, I was acting like a fanning school girl.

The whiplash I received from my emotions causing my head to spin.

"How's the food?" Pollux asked as I swallowed, clearing my throat with a forced, tight-lipped smile.

"It's amazing. Absolutely delicious."

He turned to Tatum with a triumphant smile. "See, I can do this all on my own. No need for *extra help*."

I didn't miss the way that Pollux said extra help. I knew full well what he was talking about, though they didn't know. Tatum stared at his brother, his jaw clenching as he sighed, shaking his head.

"Not with cooking, at least."

Opening my mouth to speak, I was stopped short by the opening of the back door. A figure stood within its frame, that caused my eyes to widen. There stood a woman, towering in figure, clad in leather armor with a sword strapped to her back, and massive wings that furled close behind her.

"Wow, that was quick, Kara," Tatum said smugly, pulling me from my shock.

"You called Kara?!" Pollux yelled. "Out of everyone...I can handle this..."

The woman's sharp eyes darted towards Pollux as a sneer crossed her lips. "Obviously, that isn't the case."

Stepping into the kitchen, she closed the door behind her, her dark eyes sweeping the room before finally landing on me. A small smile pulled at her lips as she stepped forward again. "Finally."

Finally, what? Who the hell is this woman?

"Uh, hi..." I responded as I glanced at Tatum. "Am I supposed to know who this is?"

He shrugged. "I don't know, do you?"

Asshole.

"I see." Kara sighed, shaking her head. "I suppose I have a lot of work ahead of me."

I wasn't sure what the hell was going on or where this creature, a woman, came from. The fact that they all seemed to communicate around me was rather unsettling and pissed me off. All I wanted was for someone to start clarifying what the hell was going on, and why my life seemed to be completely fucked up.

"Look, I don't have a clue what's going on. I understand why I'm here..." I finally said, as I internally cringed. "Well, I kind of understand...but that's beside the point. Who is this? And how long do I have to stay here? I need to keep moving."

The three of them stood there in the kitchen before me. Their eyes glued to me as I sat behind the table, the heaviness of their gaze making me feel smaller than I really was.

"Taylor, you're not going back to the life you had before," Tatum finally replied, breaking the silence.

"I have to move forward—"

"...and you will."

Kara's clipped tone quieted me as I slowly closed my mouth. The realization that my life was never going to have the possibilities it once had sunk in.

"I'm never going home, am I?" I asked, a spark of amusement in her eyes.

"You are...just to your real home, *Brina*."

Brina? Why the hell was she calling me that?

Confusion filled me as I turned my attention to Tatum, who stared at Kara with a wide-eyed, shocked expression. "What did you just say?"

Kara didn't even glance at Tatum as she turned towards Pollux. "Make me a drink and bring me something to eat. I'll wait in your office."

"Excuse me?"

She turned, making her way towards the doorway before she stopped short. "Don't question me. I used to wipe your ass, Pollux. Bring me what I asked for and tell her to come see me when she is done eating. We have much to discuss."

Once again, she spoke as if I wasn't in the room, but disappeared before I could say anything. An annoyance filled me as I realized how this situation was going to play out. My attention turned back to Tatum as I frowned, my brows furrowed, showing how annoyed I really was.

"Who the fuck was that, and why the fuck is she here?"

He popped a piece of bread into his mouth. A grin on his face as he chewed, leaning back into his chair with a small shrug of his shoulders.

"A guardian who just shared information I hadn't expected to learn."

So he didn't really know everything...what the fuck was I getting into?

CHAPTER NINETEEN

<u>Tatum</u>

Calling Kara wasn't what I had wanted to do. In fact, getting anyone else involved with what I was doing was the last thing I wanted, because it made me look incapable of handling a situation. However, my brother hadn't been the easiest person to deal with. So backup was what I had to call in. I simply found Kara the most amusing form of backup.

Especially considering she made Pollux squirm.

Taylor became quiet after the conversation between us all in the kitchen. Her eyes shifted hesitantly around the room as she slowly ate the rest of her food. A small wrinkle in between her brows as if her thoughts were more complicated than she would have liked.

"Penny for your thoughts?"

Her eyes met mine as she sipped on the orange juice in her glass. I could almost see that she wanted to say something. Her usual quick witted personality that would give me some smart remarks was unusually quiet. Placing her glass down she cleared her throat, straining a smile as she slowly stood to her feet.

"I'm fine. I think I will go and join...Kara. I believe that's what she called herself. It seems that she obviously knows more than you both do, and honestly, the way she put Pollux in his place was entertaining."

The gasp that left Pollux as I turned to find him wide-eyed with anger and shock on his face brought a chuckle to my lips. I hadn't expected her to continue being so quick-witted, but she was. She was far more extraordinary than I had initially contemplated she could be. And every moment I spent within her presence, I felt myself growing more and more attached to her being around.

Even if it was completely against how things were supposed to be.

"Sounds great. I'll come with you," I replied, my smug smile causing her to roll her eyes as she turned towards the kitchen doorway.

"You really don't have to."

"Oh," I chuckled again. "But I really do. In fact, I'm looking forward to this conversation more than you know."

She didn't bother to protest any further as she continued her way towards the living room. My feet followed behind her as Pollux finished in the kitchen. I knew he would, after all he and Kara never really saw eye to eye and the thought of getting along with her right now probably wasn't on his priority list.

I could tell right away that Kara was making herself at home. Her sword was posted against the far wall, a fire was now lit within the hearth and she sat in the arm chair, her feet rested upon the ottoman, laid back reading from a sheet of paper as if she had lived here her entire life.

"Comfortable, Kara?" I stated with amusement as her eyes lifted from the paper to me. A look of indifference crossed her gaze before she finally let the corner of her lips perk up before turning her attention to Taylor.

"Indeed. I see you're finished, Brina."

"Why do you keep calling me that?" Taylor murmured with annoyance. "My name is Taylor."

"Hmm perhaps on earth the woman may have called you that, but it isn't your name."

Kara wasn't the kind of person to so easily succumb to ignorance. She was a woman more blunt than any I had ever met and she always made a clear point to tell people exactly what was on her mind.

A woman who would give Taylor a run for her money for sure.

"Well, you can think what you want but it's not my name. My name is Taylor no matter who gave me it," Taylor replied, her arms crossed as she plopped down upon the brown leather arm chair staring at Kara. "Let's get on with it then."

A scoff of amusement left Kara as she glanced back at me with a brow raised. "Is she always like this?"

"Today's a good day." I laughed. My laughter caused Taylor to frown in disapproval though. It was clear she didn't like the way we spoke about her by the look of disdain she gave me as she sat in the chair, lips pursed and eyes narrowed.

"Tatum, go fuck yourself please. I don't need snide remarks from you."

"Ohhh—she has fire within her," I teased. Kara smiled before sitting a little straighter in her chair.

"Alright, enough both of you. It's time we get down to business," Kara replied, "there is much to talk about, and from what I can see, you are still as clueless about everything as you were the day Tatum walked into your life. Am I right?"

Taylor's eyes went wide as her lips parted slightly, just seeing her like that made my heart beat a little faster. Thoughts of her looking up at me like that made my cock twitch within my pants. It wasn't exactly proper for me to be having thoughts like this of her right now, but I couldn't help it.

Everything about who Taylor was made me feel a way I hadn't in so long.

When she finally cleared her throat with a straight face, her voice came out again, sturdy and strong but slightly less confident as she was before. "Yes, that would be correct."

"Great." Kara nodded, giving Taylor a pointed look. "Well, I suppose you should leave the attitude behind then to listen and get the answers you're looking for. I don't have the time or the patience to deal with the petulance you may have given them."

Hearing her calling Taylor out made me internally smile. The shocking look of dismay that crossed Taylors face before she quickly closed her mouth and straightened herself in her chair was beyond amusing. The woman had been a pain in my ass since I had met her, and to see her so quiet now when put in her place brought me joy.

Simply because there was no way she would act this surprised had she and I got into it.

"I understand," she finally replied, Kara's smile growing as she nodded her head to Taylor's words.

"Good. Now, I'm sure you have many questions for me. So why don't we start by you asking one, and then I'll answer. Everything else I can fill in as needed."

Twenty-one questions. It was the same game I had tried to play with Taylor and lord knows it didn't go well. Usually when she was told something she didn't want to hear, she threw a fit.

Taylor's eyes met mine as she opened and closed her mouth with a small sigh before turning her attention back to Kara. "Well, I guess we can start with why people are after me. I mean, why would the hunters be so eager to get me when there are so many other people out there. I don't understand it."

Silence fell over the room as the sounds of footsteps caused us all to turn towards the doorway. Pollux stood there, wiping his hands upon a towel before tossing it over his shoulder. "Fear. It's what drives them. They don't know how to handle change and instead of trying to understand, they seek to destroy."

Taylor's brows furrowed as she shook her head. "In today's age, that's narrow minded as hell. I mean, most of us are no different than them."

A smile crossed Kara's face as she put her feet down, sitting up in the chair she was in a little straighter. A look of understanding crossed her eyes as she glanced down for a moment and then back up to where Taylor sat.

"We have grown up in entirely different worlds, Taylor. And I may not know exactly how you feel in that aspect as my life is well defined, but you are much more special than you realize. The life and gifts you possess make you a crucial aspect of the universe, of fate."

The entire time that Kara spoke to Taylor about fate, gifts, and the universe, I couldn't take my eyes off of Taylor. It was the first time since I had met her where I realized just how confused she honestly was. How living the life she had been forced to live had made her so unable to know whether or not to trust certain aspects of her future.

A life that has left her unable to trust.

My thoughts carried me through a variety of different moments in time over the last few days that I had spent with her, to how she had reacted to everything. It was clear to me now that her response to everything did equate to that of fear. Fear that would be understanding for a person to have who had been in her situation.

Stepping back from her quietly, I turned and made my way towards the archway that leads back out into the hall. I needed a moment of quietness to gather my thoughts, but the second I stepped next to Pollux, his hand jutted out as he gripped my arm tightly. My eyes snapped to his face, his expression indifferent as he never broke gaze from where he had been staring at Taylor.

"Where do you think you're going?" he muttered, low enough only I could hear him.

I attempted to rip my arm from his grasp but failed. "Let me go. I just need a moment to myself."

My words finally snapped him from his daze as he turned his attention to me. A smirk peeked at the corner of his lips as he gently shook his head. "I had a feeling that you cared for her, Tate, but by the expression on your face, I can see that your feelings are deeper than even you realize. There is no way in hell you're walking out of this room, when your expression to everything is all the amusement I need."

"I have no idea what you're talking about, *brother*," I replied, my lip curled into a sneer of disgust. "*Now,* unhand me...or we're going to have problems."

Pollux may have been older than me, but I had always been stronger in certain ways than he was. Before I was stronger mentally. Not physically. Now, I was stronger mentally and physically. He was an old man, aged by the harsh realities of earth. I, on the other hand, still looked the part of a young man that time never touched. A man who has had opportunities to experience, not just what the world had to offer but the universe as well.

"So touchy." He chuckled. His hand released its grip as he rolled his eyes, turning his attention back to Taylor. "Just remember, she is nothing but your assignment, Tate. If you play stupid games, you win stupid prizes."

CHAPTER TWENTY

<u>**Taylor**</u>

I hadn't expected when I came here with Tate that I would be thrusted into the various amounts of crazy bullshit as I had been. My life over the past few days had become one shit show after another, but finally, I was able to gain a bit more clarity. Clarity I hadn't expected from a woman who wasn't even from this world. A woman who was more warrior than caregiver and appeared to be able to rip me apart if she had wanted to.

Her words and truths weighed heavily on me as she told me stories of what she had heard about the hunter group. How once upon a time they had actually worked with the Elder council to keep the supernaturals at bay, and a secret from the human world.

However, when Ivy was granted her powers, she lost control of herself and killed them all. Her heart broke over her mate Damian, and because of what happened, the humans that had once been friends become foes.

"So you're saying that Ivy lost herself in her powers and the humans saw it?" I asked, trying to clarify what Kara had just told me. Because it didn't make sense why they would suddenly be scared when they had already been okay with our world.

"Yes, but that was because they had never seen anything like her. Ivy wasn't just a supernatural creature. She was the daughter of Odin. A celestial power and pregnant, though that was another story on its own. The loss of her mate caused her to change, her heart broken with the absence of his presence. An absence the humans helped to create."

My heart broke for Ivy hearing the story. A woman who had everything taken from her and all because she was different. It was a feeling I could relate to. No one had ever really wanted me in my life, and my mother and sister only wanted to control me.

Which was why I avoided them at all costs.

"I can't imagine losing the person I love most. I don't think I could live—"

My words died off as my mind went to Deidra, and everything that had happened to her. The hurt and pain resurfacing as I tried to fight back the tears that threatened to fall.

"That wasn't the end of their story, Brina," Kara said, her words causing me to glance up at her in confusion.

"What do you mean?"

Her eyes moved towards Pollux and Tatum, who had turned the corner with a drink in his hands as his gaze landed upon me. "I mean that love saved him and brought him back from death."

"That's not possible…is it?" I asked as I turned my attention back to Kara. A twinkle of amusement in her eyes as she shrugged her shoulders.

"I don't know…why don't you tell me?"

Her words confused me. The way she said it was as if she was implying I knew something, but of course, I didn't. I didn't have the first clue as to what she was talking about, but then again, I didn't miss the glance she was giving me as if I was supposed to.

"Kara, how would I know? I wasn't there."

"Are you sure?" Again, her words confused me. My brows knitted together as I sat speechless, staring at her unable to understand why it was that she would think that I had been there. From the sounds of it, this had happened long long ago and there was no way that I had been present.

"I'm pretty sure," I muttered, glancing towards Tatum and Pollux, who stared at me silently before I turned my attention back to Kara. "Why would you think I was?"

Shrugging her shoulders, she chuckled softly. "Because you were, Brina. You were the one who granted the woman's wish to restore her mate."

Her words hit me like a brick wall. My mind tried to process what she said but the only way I could was with an abrupt amount of laughter. The kind of laughter that was unexpected and when I tried to stop, it just made it worse.

"Do you really think that I'm going to believe that?"

Kara rolled her eyes with a heavy sigh. "And here I thought we were on the right track."

"Well, you thought wrong. I wasn't there. It's not possible."

"And yet it is," she snipped back. "You're the Phoenix, Brina. The goddess of life and death. The Elder Hallow of the Fae realm, the source of power between worlds."

Again, with the dramatics of me being a source of power.

The three of them were adamant on making me believe what they were saying, and as much as I wanted to keep telling them they are crazy...I was slowly starting to wonder if there really was truth behind what they were saying.

"I know this is a lot for you to process," Kara began, her voice calm and steady as I stared at her with apprehension.

"A lot?" I piped up. "That's an understatement."

"I already told you if you have questions to ask."

A scoff echoed from the doorway caused Kara and I both to turn and look at Pollux, who seemed more annoyed than anything. His arms crossed across his chest as if the entire situation was nothing more than an inconvenience.

Since I got here, Pollux had been nothing but a pain in my ass. I know I wasn't the easiest person to be around, but dealing with him hurt me more than anything. Because every time I saw him, I was reminded of the night I lost Deidra.

The night that I lost the last person who truly loved me.

"Actually, I do have a question..." I stated, my eyes locking with Pollux. "How did Deidra fit into all of this? And why did she keep everything a secret?"

I watched as Pollux's angry scowl fell into a look of sadness. His eyes softened as his shoulders dropped, his stance becoming more wavering than rigid. I knew the moment I got here that the angry persona that Pollux gave off was just a front, but I had ignored it because of my anger. I had assumed that he was the villain and honestly, I didn't remember quite what had happened that night.

What if everything I had thought was accurate had actually been wrong.

"Would you like to tell her Pollux?" Kara said with confidence, her words pulled me from my thoughts as I focused on the question she had asked.

"He knows?" I muttered, "wait...you know?"

He quickly corrected his posture as he cleared his throat. His mouth opened and closed as if he was going to say something but instead, he turned and walked away. The silence that fell between us was awkward and as I turned my attention back to Kara. I could almost see the wheels turning in her mind. As if she knew all the secrets of the world and was simply waiting for them to play out.

As she turned her gaze to me from the empty doorway she smiled a soft sigh escaping her lips as she shook her head. "I suppose I will tell you what I know."

"Now do you see why I called you here?" Tatum's voice was unexpected, but it wasn't unwelcomed. Something about his voice seemed to calm me, and though I got irritated with him every now and again...I really liked him being around.

In fact, I loved him being around me.

"Yes, yes. I can see that, Tatum. Sit down and let me tell the girl what she needs to know. We don't have time for long drawn out stories."

"Yes, ma'am." His sarcastic and quick witted response earned him a glare from Kara, who didn't seem pleased by the way he addressed her. A sneer crossed her lips only for a moment as she turned to me.

"Deidra was the daughter of a very powerful woman. A wiccan named Samalia. She was the guardian of the Phoenix temple, and within the temple, they helped reunite your former lives with new life. A cycle that was interrupted when Moria killed them all, including Somalia, allowing her to steal you and raise you as her own."

My heart dropped hearing what Kara said. My mother, though often a cruel woman, had killed an entire group of people to take me for herself. I had known that she was capable of horrible things, but I never could imagine her doing something like that.

It was completely drastic, and out of character for her.

"No, that—" I gasped as I shook my head.

"Yes, Brina. Stop avoiding the truth. The night that Moira helped the hunters attack the cabin, she killed Deidra as well, just to prove a point..."

"Would you stop calling me Brina!" I yelled, my anger flaring as a warm rush of power seemed to course through me as I jumped to my feet."My name is Taylor!"

I didn't understand why I was so angry about what she said, but clenching my fists at my side, I felt the wave of hatred flow over my skin that made me want to burn the world down. The familiar feeling caused my mind to wander, a pain radiating in my chest that made me feel like the world had opened a void there. A void that could never be fixed or filled, a hurt that was like nothing else I'd ever felt.

"Taylor, you have to calm down," Tatum said, my eyes unable to focus on anything other than Kara and the hatred I felt. Not for her, but for everything.

Holding back a gasp, I tried to push away the feelings I had, tears finally sliding down my face as I tried to hold myself together. "I'm sorry, I can't anymore today. I need some air."

I moved from the living room as fast as my feet would take me. I wasn't sure where I was going, but I moved straight for the front door and inhaled the fresh crisp scent of mother nature the moment I closed the front door behind me.

Tears slid down my face as I tried to calm my racing heart. My life was completely fucked in so many ways, and I wasn't sure how the hell I was going to be able to accept this. To accept the truth of what they were saying because I couldn't deny it anymore.

I was the Elder Hallow, or whatever the fuck they wanted to call me.

I wasn't a succubus, and my entire life was nothing but a fucking lie.

Tatum

The moment she stormed out of the room, Kara stood to her feet as if to go after Taylor. Something I knew wouldn't go over well considering that she had been the one to give Taylor the bad news.

"Um, maybe I should go check on her instead of you."

"But I'm her guardian..." Kara said with confidence, her brows furrowed as she seemed confused as to why I would make such a comment.

"Yes, I know, but so am I. She doesn't know you, Kara. Let me do it instead."

Kara was silent for a moment before letting out a heavy breath, and she nodded. "Very well. Do what you have to, but we need to finish. We have to get back."

Nodding, I turned and made my way out as Taylor had done. If I was going to help bring her around to everything that had been going on, I was going to have to find some common ground with her.

The way her eyes fell as Kara told her the truth tore at a part of me. My heart felt heavy for her as she realized how deep everything went. And it was just the tip of it all. She has no idea how important she is to the universe and how chaotic things have been since she had been gone.

Making my way outside, I walked the grounds searching for where she could have gone. It wasn't until I walked around the back of the manor that my eyes finally fell on her tiny form outside the greenhouse, admiring the plants that Trixie had once been so fond of.

There was a grace in her movements, a delicate dance between strength and fragility as she seemed to admire the plants that still managed to survive the neglect of the homeowner and the harsh disadvantages of mother nature. Her fingers caressed the soft yellow hues that decorated the petals as if she hadn't just been told the most harsh realities of her life.

Every line and curve spoke of a life well-lived, of experiences etched into the tapestry of her being. In that moment, time stood still, and I found myself awestruck by her mere presence.

I longed to be a part of her world, to share in her journey of self-discovery. I wanted to be the one to stand beside her, offering support and encouragement as she faced life's challenges with unwavering grace. I wasn't sure why I felt the way I did, but it was as if fate announced a new path for me, and I wasn't going to be one to refuse it like Pollux.

She turned, her eyes meeting mine, and I saw a spark of recognition, a connection forged through time that was never meant to be broken.

"You didn't have to come out here to check on me," she said softly, her arms crossing over her chest as if she was cold. She wore vulnerability like a coat that made me internally promise to always protect her.

She may have been a succubus, a creature of the night that preyed on men.

But it wasn't who she truly was.

"I wanted to," I confessed with a small smile. "I'm sorry how that was all put on you like that. I didn't know how much you weren't told."

Her eyes widened slightly as her lips parted. "You didn't know I didn't know all of that?"

Hesitating, I sighed, thinking over my words carefully. "Not everything, no. I had my suspicions when I first met you that you didn't know who you really were."

Nodding her head, she stayed quiet for a moment. Which surprised me because usually she was very vocal when it came to being upset. Her eyes scanned the greenhouse, a faint hint of joy seemed to cross her brilliant Cerulean blue eyes. "I don't want to talk about that shit anymore, Tate. I know that's why you're out here."

"That's okay, we don't have to right now," I replied. Kara had made it clear I needed to get her back, but seeing her calm right now or at least seemingly calm was something I didn't get to see often.

"This place is beautiful. I take it that it belonged to his wife?"

"Yeah. Trixie is actually a pixie who loved everything that pertained to nature. It was her gift."

Her eyes darted back to mine in confusion. "She's a pixie?"

"Yeah."

"Oh, I thought she was fae," she replied, before looking back.

"She is. Fae is like a generalized word. There are many types of races within that category. Sort of like with humans, I suppose."

Again, she turned to me with a wary look but this time she chuckled with a nod. "Whatever you say, mystery man."

"Mystery man?"

Her mouth snapped shut at her words as she seemed to close down. I wasn't sure what had transpired there, but one thing was for sure, I would never be able to get enough of her smile and laughter. When she wasn't being crazy and acting like everyone was out to get her, she was a joy to be around.

"Hey, it's okay," I finally spoke up, trying to break the uncomfortable silence. "If you want to call me your mystery man, I'm fine with it."

"My mystery man?" she replied in a teasing tone as she stepped closer to me, a sense of seductiveness washing over her. "I didn't know you were mine."

I didn't have the slightest clue what had happened. I had literally just watched this girl crumble and then bounce back like nothing had happened. Not that I was complaining. The way she was acting right now had my cock throbbing with anticipation. "Uh, I was just making a joke."

No! My internal mind seemed to scream as I watched Taylor roll her eyes and step away. The moment instantly killed with me opening my big fucking mouth.

All I could think about was when I had her in the bathroom. Her body writhing as I brought her to the edge and tipped her over. The way she tasted on my tongue as she came—the sweet taste of honey.

A flavor I had been craving for ever since.

"Well, thanks for coming to check on me. I think I just want to wander around for a bit. Kind of take my mind off things."

Take her mind off things? God, please let me take your mind off things.

Thinking over what she said, an idea came to mind, and an opportunity for me to get to know her better. After all, if I was going to be stuck with her, I might as well use the time to get to know her more. Figure out what kind of person she truly was. She would definitely need someone on her side once we got to Asgard.

"Well, I know a place."

"You do?" she asked, one brow raised as she stared at me with skepticism.

"Yeah, I do. A place I used to go to as a kid. I think you will like it."

Taylor seemed wary of my proposal at first before reluctantly giving in with a small nod. Her hand gestured for me to lead the way. I shook my head and stepped behind her, gesturing towards the woods.

"Where are you going? You're not going to lead me to the woods to kill me now are you?"

Laughter escaped me. I glanced over my shoulder at her walking warily behind me. "Now, where would the fun be in that after all the trouble I went through to get you here in the first place."

CHAPTER TWENTY-ONE

<u>Taylor</u>

Going into a forest with Tatum wasn't exactly what I had expected when he said he wanted to show me something. In fact, a million and one different situations played through my head as I contemplated if he was leading me to my death. Even though that was completely stupid.

I hadn't missed the way the bulge in the front of his pants hardened when I had stepped towards him. Every part of me wanted him to fuck me to oblivion right there in the damn garden.

The farther we ventured through the woods, the more the dappling sunlight filtered through the thick canopy, a sense of anticipation mingled with the fluttering of my heart. I was alone with him after having fantasized this morning about the multitude of things I had wanted him to do to me, and because of that, I couldn't help but feel conflicting emotions being around him.

Despite those feelings, I followed him. My steps echoed his, the crisp earth beneath our feet whispering secrets of magic that filled the grounds of this land.

"So, what is this place?" I asked, a playful glint in my eyes as I nudged him gently with my elbow. "Is it a magical place?"

He chuckled, his laughter carrying on the breeze and intertwining with the melodic birdsong that serenaded our journey. "Something like that," he replied, his voice laced with a hint of mischief. "It may just be the place you need to help you connect with a past you long forgot."

I rolled my eyes, a smile tugging at the corners of my lips. "If only my situation were that easy. If that were the case, I'm pretty sure your brother would have tried to drown me there already in an attempt to help me remember."

"Do you think I would really allow him to do something like that?"

Laughter snorted from my throat as I shrugged my shoulders, picking up a stick from the forest floor before tossing it off into the nearby brush. "I'm sure you would agree with him. After all, I have been nothing but a pain in your ass."

He feigned offense, placing a hand dramatically over his heart. "You wound me," he said, a twinkle of amusement in his eyes. "Pain in the ass or not, I take my job very seriously."

I laughed, the sound bubbling forth like a spring of joy. There was a lightness to our banter, an ease that filled the air between us as we continued our trek through the woods towards whatever place he had set in mind. Something about being here with him was rather comforting. Like I had been here in the past, and was reuniting with old friends.

"So, how far away is this place?" I asked, curiosity tugging at my voice.

He glanced at me, his gaze warm and genuine. "Not too far away," he replied, his tone earnest. "Are you not enjoying the walk? You said you wanted to clear your mind."

Stunned by his admission, I went to speak but the sound of rushing water grew louder, its melody guiding us closer to our destination, distracting me from my reply. My eyes darted towards him only to find him expectant of the noise.

With a simple gesture of his hand, I pushed ahead of him, breaking through the brush and treeline to a lake that sat within the woods. It didn't seem like much but the cool water glistened from the sun's rays that shone upon it through the canopies. The rocks stacked high to one side with a small creek-like fall that flowed down in a majestic manner.

It was simple, but it was breathtaking. A lone body of water tucked away from the harsh realities of the world. A solitude of security for all animal life that inhabited the woods around us. "What is this place?"

"It doesn't have a name, but it was a place that I visited frequently when I resided in this pack."

"It's beautiful," I muttered as I stepped forward toward the water's edge. Gently bending, I dipped my fingers into the cool embrace of the lake, a surge of calmness washing through me, radiating from my fingertips to my heart.

"You know," I began, my voice soft and earnest, "all these years I spent running from everyone and everything. I always felt like I didn't belong, and now I'm starting to really wonder if a lot of the shit I went through wasn't because of my mother, or well, Moira."

Turning to him, he stared at me with a look of understanding. As if to say he knew how I felt or at least understood why I would feel the way I did. "I can help you figure out who you are, Taylor. You don't have to go through it alone."

"Why do you want to help me? You don't even know me."

Stepping closer to me, he frowned, shaking his head. "I don't have to know you to want to help you. You deserve so much more than the hateful life you have been given."

I found myself standing face to face with him, our eyes locked in an intense gaze. The air crackled with a palpable tension, like a dance of desire and curiosity, a delicate balance teetering on the edge of surrender. A surrender I so desperately wanted to give into since the moment I saw him. The simple taste of what he had given me in the bathroom wasn't enough, I wanted him to fill me. Stretch me till I was screaming his name.

"I don't know what to say..." I admitted, my heart all but beating out of my chest.

Chuckling, he reached out, his fingers brushing against my cheek, sending a shiver down my spine. I could feel the heat emanating from his touch, igniting a fire within me that I couldn't ignore. "Then don't say anything, my lady."

His words were like whispers on the delicate wind that flowed around us, his lips inching closer to me by the second. Soft and inviting, they hovered just inches from mine. The anticipation grew within me with each passing second. The unspoken desire hung heavy in the air around us, as I watched the hunger in his eyes grow, mirroring my own.

"What are you waiting for," I whispered. My lips gently brushed his own.

"For you to beg for the release you need."

I had done a lot of things in my life, but begging was never one of them. Though, I needed what he was willing to give me. I needed the release, the promise of unimaginable desire. I needed him like a fire needed a flame.

"Please," I gasped. "Help me remember."

With a surge of boldness, I closed the remaining distance, pressing my lips against his. The connection ignited a spark between us as he pulled me close, his arm wrapped around my waist as he held me to him. The hunger in his kiss only deepened, as the fire of pleasure burned between my thighs.

The heat between us intensified, a crescendo of desire that drowned out the world around us. There was only him and me, lost in the depths of our own carnal desires. Desires that slowly grew into an insatiable hunger, a whirlwind of passion and longing that I hadn't realized that I needed.

"I need more," I groaned against his lips. My fingers pulled at the fabric of his shirt, pleading for contact with his skin. For anything to dull the ache in my core, desperate to be fucked into submission.

Tatum didn't waste time. Bending down, he gripped the backs of my thighs, lifting me up as he walked me towards the smooth rock formations on the edge of the pool. His lips broke from mine as he set me down. "Are you sure about this? Once I take you, there is no going back."

I didn't have the slightest clue what he meant, but I nodded my head, regardless. I pulled my shirt over my head, tossing it to the side, letting my perky breasts spill out in full display for him. I never really cared for bras, and right now, I was glad for that because the way his eyes darkened let me know right away how badly he wanted me. Especially when he lowered his mouth, catching my erect nipples between his lips, causing me to gasp before letting them free once more.

"Take me in any way that you want," I gasped. He stepped forward, removing his shirt before pulling at the hem of my pants.

"Are you sure you want to give me that kind of power?" he growled, a hint of smirk across his lips as he watched me.

"Yes, I do."

Tatum was a man who had ignited a flame deep within me, drawing me closer with every passing second that I spent with him. I couldn't take my eyes off him as the rest of our clothes disappeared. The long thick cock between his thighs caused my mouth to salivate with a desire to taste him.

However, it was quite clear I wouldn't get the chance for that. At least not this time around.

He stepped towards me, a flicker of desire danced in his eyes. A primal hunger that made me curious as the man he was. From what I guessed, seeing as he was related to a shifter family, he wasn't anymore. Instead, he was something different. And the power that I tasted that night at the rest area was something I craved for again.

I was captivated by the sight of him. His lean well built physique wasn't like most men that I had been with before. He wasn't piled with huge muscles, instead they were there, well defined with a perfectly sculpted six pack that trailed down to lines that curved towards his erected cock.

There was no hesitation in his movements. His hand placed against the stone next to my head as he hovered over me, his teeth nipping at my lip before he kissed me again. His fingers brushed down the side of my face before dipping down over the curve of my neck, towards the delicate peaks of my breasts.

He grasped my nipples between his fingers, rolling them, the feeling of pain and pleasure like lightning through my body causing me to gasp into his kiss. Slowly, his lips moved from mine, down over my jawline and over the curves of my neck, latching onto my nipple. His tongue swirled around, causing a pool of desire to build within me before the bliss was released and his lips continued traveling south as he teased me.

More. I wanted more. His mouth latched onto my core like it had before. I moaned in pleasure, my back arched and my legs spread wide giving him full access. He consumed me with a fury that I hadn't expected.

"Oh god," I cried out as he brought me closer to the edge. "Please, Tatum, I can't take it anymore. I need you."

As if my words pulled him from the hunger induced rage he was in while he feasted upon me, his eyes met mine and to his feet he came. The head of his cock lined with my entrance, his hand guiding it inside me. Stretching me more than I have ever been, to a point I didn't think I could continue.

There wasn't a time for words as his lips crashed upon mine again. His thrusts, not gentle, rocked my body. His hips slammed into mine as he held me tight, the pure primal aggression of his claim tipping me closer and closer to the edge.

Time ceased to exist. The world faded away, leaving only us, entwined in a fiery embrace. Every touch, every caress, sent a surge of electricity coursing through me, setting my skin ablaze. Even the rock beneath my back sent a pleasurable sensation through my body as he fucked me like I had never been fucked before.

Our bodies pressed against each other, aligning in a rhythm that far surpassed that of what I would consider normal. The grunts and groans of the pleasure we created within each other echoed around the forest as we pushed each other to the edge until there was nothing more stopping us from spilling over.

With a scream of pleasure, the ecstasy of our union ripped from me as he slammed himself into me once more. His hands held me as close as possible as he stilled, spilling every inch of him inside me. His warmth enveloped me, and I melted into his embrace, craving more of his touch, more of the pleasure he effortlessly bestowed upon me.

On the edge of this secret lake, we lost ourselves in the intoxication of our union. The passion we shared overtook us, a force greater than anything we had ever experienced.

"Are you okay?" he whispered against my lips as he stared down at me with an edge of concern in his gaze.

I was confused by his question. Unsure of why he would ask me something like that, but with a soft chuckle, I nodded. "Of course I am. I'm better than okay. Why do you ask?"

Slipping himself from me, I sat up as he held out his hand to lead me into the cool waters of the lake. "As I'm sure you may know, I'm not a shifter like my brother anymore. What I am can be dangerous. I don't want to hurt you."

"Oh," I replied with a nod. "Well, you don't have to worry about that with me. I'm not sure you could hurt me if you wanted to. I'm stronger than I look."

Slipping into the water, he pulled me to him again, holding me up within the depths of the lake. In his arms, I found solace in the passion that defied the logic of who I was. In his arms, he ignited a flame inside me that I didn't know had been extinguished. A familiarity that I didn't know I craved.

"Well then, next time we'll have to try something new."

His words weren't a suggestion. They were a warning—a promise—of what was to come and that was something I was definitely looking forward to.

CHAPTER

Twenty-Two

The day spent with Tatum at the lake was more than I could have ever asked for. As much as we both wanted to stay there, we knew we had to get back to the pack house as night was slowly setting in. The last thing we wanted was for Pollux to think we had left the pack lands.

Even though I wish I fucking had.

Not to mention, Kara was waiting.

The moment between us in the woods was gone when we stepped foot into the pack house. We were greeted by the sour expression of Pollux, who looked between us as if knowing exactly what had happened. Never in my life had I felt like a schoolgirl who got caught red-handed.

And it only got worse when Kara walked around the corner with her arms crossed over her chest, and a brow raised as she glanced between Tatum and me.

"Take care of things, huh?" she murmured, "at least it brought her back."

Oh my god, what?!

"I'm going upstairs... you guys—" I gasped as I looked at the three of them. "Have fun with whatever...this is."

I made my way upstairs not wasting another second staying in their presence while they talked about whatever it was they had to talk about. The uncomfortable silence that had fallen over us at her words was enough to make me want to leave with haste.

Not to mention, I really needed to clean the dirt off my body.

Thirty minutes later and a long hot shower, my eyes locked onto my phone as a notification alert caught my attention. The flashing red light caused my stomach to drop as I opened and closed my mouth, hesitant on what I was going to find.

Taking a deep breath, I picked it up, noticing the low battery and my sister's name across the screen. My heart dropped into my stomach as I quickly pressed the message, expecting only the worst from her.

I told you this would happen. We are on our way to save you. Mother needs you home, and this time, it's best you stay in place.

"They're on their way?" I whispered, as confusion filled me as I read her message over again. "Shit...this is not good."

Slipping on a pair of shorts and a tank top, I yanked my bedroom door only to come face to face with Tatum, whose fist was raised as if he was preparing to knock.

"Tatum..." I murmured as he stared down at me with the same intense gaze he had before. "What are you doing here?"

"I was coming to check on you. But it seems you were going somewhere."

Nodding, I stepped aside, letting him into my room as I closed the door behind him. "Yeah, my sister just texted me and said they were coming here. That my mother wants me home—"

"What?!" he all but shouted, his eyes a blaze as he spun to face me. "What text...you have your phone?"

I hadn't realized my phone was an issue, nor had he asked me about it before. I pulled it from my pocket and handed it to him. His eyes gazed over the message my sister had sent before he crumbled my phone in his hand like it was nothing. The pieces fell to the floor at my feet as my mouth hung open wide.

"What the hell was that for?!"

Shaking his head, he furrowed his gaze at me with a frown. "They can track you with your phone, Taylor. How could you be so fucking stupid!"

Shocked by his outburst, I found myself speechless as I stared at him, eyes wide in disbelief. Not only had he yelled at me, but he was telling me I was stupid as if I would have considered my phone being an issue. He had forgotten that he was the one who dragged me into this, knowing I didn't know what I was doing. I had lived a somewhat peaceful life the last few years, and had never considered that someone could track me through my phone.

Did that make me naive...I suppose so. But it wasn't like I did it on purpose.

"I'm sorry," I snapped. My eyes cast towards the floor as I crossed my arms over my chest. "I didn't think about that."

"You know what...don't worry about it. I'll fucking handle it." His tone was nothing but angry, laced with the irritation he felt in that moment. My eyes connected with his as I saw disappointment looming there, disappointment that completely crushed me as I realized how I had royally fucked up.

No matter how much I may have fucked up, he was also in the wrong. The once sensitive side of me quickly disappeared as I narrowed my gaze at him crossing my arms over my chest. "Go fuck yourself, Tatum."

"Excuse me?" he sneered, fists clenched at his sides. "Go fuck myself?!"

"Your heard me. You're sitting here angry at me, but you forget, I didn't know what the fuck was going on with anything! It's the twenty-first century. Why didn't you bother to ever ask me about a fucking cellphone? You should have known I probably had one!"

He was quiet for a moment as his sneer disappeared, and his lips instead met into a thin tight line. "Like I said, I'll handle it."

The weight of guilt pressed heavily upon my heart as I watched Tatum turn and leave my room, the door slamming behind him. I should have known not to do what I did, but I wasn't thinking like I should have and stupidly caused issues.

Now on top of everything else, he was upset with me. I wasn't sure why it bothered me so much but it did, and as much as I didn't want to show I was bothered. I couldn't stop the single tear from escaping my eye, running down my cheek.

If I was going to make it at all in this new life I was going to have to stop my foolish behavior and become more than I was. I couldn't just ignore the seriousness of my situation, and deep down, I wished that there was someone or something that could guide me.

My mind instantly drifted to Kara, and the words of wisdom she had provided before.

Maybe in the morning, I needed to do what I should have and actually listen for once.

I drifted into a deep slumber, letting my mind slip into darkness as I sought solace for myself not found within the mundane world. However, the darkness seemed to have other plans and eventually, I ended upon grassy turf seeking clarity through my foggy white surroundings.

As I continued to stare into the fog, it slowly lifted. My eyes focused on a sight that I hadn't ever expected to see. All around me lay a vast, ethereal forest, where the trees whispered secrets to one another, their branches reaching skyward like ancient sentinels, wrapping around the white pillared rocks of run down temples.

Even the air was tinged with an otherworldly aura, and as a gentle breeze brushed against my skin, I felt at peace. The same kind of peace one would find in a place they called home.

I hadn't the slightest clue where I was or what was going on. But as I stood from where I had been lying, I felt a pull towards the grand stairs that seemed to reach towards the sky, beckoning me forth as if something or someone was waiting.

Step by step, I ventured forward through the mist until my surroundings began to shift. Shadows danced within the crevasses of the stone statues and buildings, creating a mesmerizing play of light and dark. The path ahead became obscured until a figure emerged from the mist at the top of the steps.

The figure of a man stood tall and proud, his attire otherworldly as he stood in what looked like Nordic clothing of brown furs and gray linen. Yet, with a shimmer to them as if the time in which we stood wasn't the time in which he belonged.

"Hello?"

My greeting went unacknowledged as he seemed to stare at me, his eyes shimmering with a wisdom beyond time, and a smile that spoke of the stories he had told for centuries.

"Brina," he called, his voice resonated through the stillness of the ruins. The name echoed in my ears, awakening something deep within my soul. "Brina, the keeper of life and death."

I hesitated, my heart pounding with anticipation and curiosity.

Why does everyone keep calling me Brina?

"My name is Taylor," I called out, trying to keep my mind focused. A sharp pain in the back of my head caused my eyes to burn with the desire to close them.

"You have been called many things over the years, my child. However, you will always be my Brina."

Okay, so the old guy doesn't listen, I'll run with that.

"Who are you?" I managed to ask, my voice barely above a whisper. The words seemed to get lost in the haze of confusion being created by the thrum of power surrounding us. A power that seemed to flow from him and reach out to me.

As if it had missed me.

The man's eyes held mine, his gaze piercing through the veils of time. "So it is true what they say then. You do not remember who you truly are?"

Shaking my head, I found it hard to reply as my knee bent and I dropped down, a sharp cry escaping my lips as I tried to find the will to stand once more. "Please, I can't take the pain anymore."

"Pain?" he replied, furrowing his brow as I finally closed my eyes. The sounds of his footsteps approaching caught me off guard, but not as much as when his hand touched the back of my head, instantly relieving the pain and pressure.

"What are you doing?" I gasped in relief, my eyes opening to face him as he stared down at me with a dark depth I hadn't seen before.

"This place isn't made for curses, Brina. Your mind is begging for release, and I am simply releasing the pressure that has been building."

The moment his touch disappeared, he held out his hand, helping me to my feet. One would have expected to be afraid of a man like this, or perhaps uncertain of whether or not to trust him. But not me. I did trust him, and I didn't understand why.

"Are you a god or something?"

He chuckled with a nod as he led me towards a small seating area at the top of the stairs. "I am Balder, son of Odin, and the embodiment of immortality," he replied, his voice a gentle melody that wove itself into my being. "I have been waiting for you, Brina, for you to come back to me. For you to remember the power inside you that has long been forgotten. A power that can restore balance to our fractured worlds. You are my daughter, a secret I kept for thousands of years. Stolen from me by those who seek to abuse your gifts."

His words stirred something within me, awakening a sense of purpose I had never known. I had always felt a connection to something greater than myself, a yearning to explore a need to be free. However, I never knew how to obtain it.

"I don't understand," I confessed, looking to him for clarity. "I'm sleeping right now. Surely this is just made up within my mind?"

"Made up?" He bellowed with laughter. "Not entirely."

"Not entirely? Now you're making me feel crazy, and you keep calling me your child. How am I your daughter? I mean, maybe I'm having serious daddy issues going on right now and my mind is creating these situations.

"No, no," he replied with amusement. "You are my daughter, Brina. Hasn't Kara explained everything to you yet?"

Opening my mouth, I quickly snapped it shut and grimaced causing him to laugh.

"I see. You know you should probably listen to her."

I rolled my eyes with a sigh. "Yeah, I'm kind of figuring that out. There is just so much I don't understand. I'm supposed to be a succubus—"

"No, you're not," he snapped, catching me off guard. A dark glimpse of something shadowed within the depth of his eyes before quickly disappearing. "You're not a succubus, Brina. That is what they told you because of the powers you possess. You are not one of those creatures, it's why you don't do the things they do. It's why you don't find pleasure in killing or have the need to feed like they do."

"So I really am the Elder Hallow?" It was a question I had never asked myself before.

However, Balder gazed upon me with pure joy in his eyes as the corner of his lips turned up into a smile. "You're the daughter of Fate, Brina. You are the Elder Hallow, a source of power and protection that has the ability to change one's destiny."

"I'm what—but Tatum—" I stammered as he raised a hand to brush a strand of hair behind my ear. A gentle touch that made me feel safe and loved even in my dream.

"Tatum is the only man that you need to trust until you are returned to our world. Danger is coming for you, Brina. You must warn them to prepare."

CHAPTER
TWENTY-THREE

Taylor

Jolted from sleep, my heart pounded erratically. My mind fogged over from my restless slumber, sweat beading down my forehead as I tried to catch my breath. The remnants of my crazy dream still lingered in my mind, its images swirling like a chaotic storm brewing off the coast of some small island.

Balder. The name lingered on my lips. A man—no, a god—had come to see me. A god who claimed to be my father. I wanted more than anything to dismiss the entire thing, chalking it up to an overactive imagination, but I couldn't.

The urgency to tell Tatum what had happened far surpassed anything else I could want in that moment.

Twisted within the sheets and blankets of my bed, I untangled myself and rushed towards the door. I threw it open and stormed across the hall to speak with Tatum. The only problem was he wasn't there. His pitch black room was silent, and his bed untouched showed no signs that he had been there at all.

However, his lingering scent washed around me when I opened his door. My heart beat as if I could feel him touching my skin right then. A memory of the way he doted on me all afternoon as if I was the only person he wanted to be with.

The thoughts of how his body caressed every inch of me as he took me over and over again on that rock in the woods. His lips over my nipples as he filled me like no one ever had.

Forcing myself back to the present, I backed out of his room, closing the door before heading down the stairs in search of Tatum. I had to tell him what the man in my dream said, even if I didn't want to believe it. I had too. Something about it was real. Something I couldn't let go of.

Though after the fight we had just had over the entire situation, I found myself nervous. Nervous about whether he would even listen to me.

Compelled by an indomitable instinct, I descended the staircase, my bare feet making little sound against the polished wood. I rushed into the office, my eyes connected with Pollux and Tatum, their faces etched with lines of concern, mirroring the weight of responsibility about whatever they were discussing.

"Tatum," I called out, causing them both to turn towards me.

"Taylor..." Tatum stated, his brows furrowed for a moment before becoming relaxed.

"I need to speak to you."

He hesitated for a moment as he glanced toward Pollux, who seemed disinterested as he continued to look over a large piece of parchment on his desk. "I'll be right back."

Pollux grumbled as Kara walked back into the room. Her eyes raked over my form as she made her way towards the desk. Tatum didn't hesitate to walk straight towards me as he pulled me towards the doorway of the office.

"Is everything okay?" he asked, his voice low and a concerned expression etched across his face as he narrowed his brows and stepped towards me. "I really don't have time for this right now."

"Yeah, I know. I just needed to speak with you privately for a moment."

"Okay, well what do you need?" he asked harshly. The difference in his tone from how he had spoken to me before took me by surprise. It was clear that whatever he and his brother had been talking about was tense, but I hadn't expected him to speak to me the way he had.

"I had a dream—"

"Taylor," he replied, cutting me off. "You stopped our conversation for a dream?"

My mouth dropped open as I tried to understand what his problem was. "You didn't even let me finish—"

He sighed as he hung his head for a moment before he turned to me. "Look, I'm sorry I keep snapping at you, and we can talk about this after, I promise. But right now, I have to focus because we have serious problems coming our way, and I need to help protect this pack."

Closing my mouth, I stood taken aback once more. It was clear that he did have serious problems on his hand and as much as I wanted to tell him, I didn't want to burden him. I mean, what Balder told me to tell them—technically they already knew.

They knew that trouble was coming so me telling them wouldn't be new.

Nodding, I gave him a forced smile and watched as he turned back towards where Pollux and Kara were speaking in hushed whispers. Conversations that I obviously wasn't permitted to be part of. Which upset me even more since Balder had told me that I needed to stay close to Tatum. That Tatum would keep me safe.

But he was right. With them coming, he did need to protect the pack.

***

I wasn't sure how much time had passed since I had tried to speak to Tatum. I ended up roaming the upstairs rooms until I found the quiet shell of a library that looked to have been vacant for some time. The floral wallpaper, and cloth covered tables spoke of its abandonment and yet for some reason, there was an air of life that still resided here.

"I wondered how long it would take for you to find this place."

Kara's voice took me by surprise as I glanced up to see her tall imposing figure fit tightly within the door frame. Her dark eyes took me in as her wings fit snuggly, tucked behind her back as she entered the room.

"What do you mean?" I asked, unsure why she thought I would even find this place to begin with.

"There is a lot you don't know about this pack, or the family that has tried to protect it, Brina. But one thing that has never changed over time is this room. It was passed down from one Luna to another, time after time. The air of the goddesses' powers still linger within every crevice of this room, in every page of the books on the shelves."

I watched as she walked around the room, her fingers trailing over the books upon the shelves as if remembering things from long ago. Her eyes trailing over every inch of a past that I wasn't privy to.

"How long have you spent with these people?" I asked softly. "The way you talk... it's like you have spent a century."

She let a small laugh escape her lips as she slowly turned to face me. "Brina, there is much you don't remember but I promise you... you will remember very soon."

I scoffed, shaking my head with a small grin, "I doubt that. I feel like all I keep doing is fucking things up."

"Perhaps, but he will forgive you. You're bound to him."

"First off, ouch." I smiled at her as I watched her shrug her shoulders.

'Lying isn't something I'm partial to, Brina. I will always be blunt." She replied, a sense of honesty in her words I had never really felt with anyone. Well, almost anyone. My mind slowly drifting to Tatum, and the way he tried to tell me things countless times, but I had been to stupid to fucking listen.

"Do you really think he will forgive me?"

She nodded, "in time."

"Time has never really been on my side, Kara." I replied, reminding myself that eventually time ends for everyone.

She stepped towards me with an almost motherly expression in her eyes that I hadn't expected. "Time, Brina. Will always be on your side, and in your favor. Never forget that it is you who decides when time begins and when it comes to an end."

<u>Tatum</u>

The moon hung high in the ink-black sky, casting an eerie glow over the dense forest surrounding the pack lands. The scent of damp earth mingled with the musk of the pack as if nature itself held its breath in anticipation.

The hunters were at our borders, and the future of this pack rested in our hands. The magic that flowed here was strong, created from remnants of the powers my mother once possessed. But there was only so much protection it would give us and there was no telling what tactics the hunters had that could potentially destroy everything.

Pollux stood beside me, his gaze fixed on the horizon where danger lurked within the shadows just outside of the barrier to our lands. His broad shoulders were tense, excluding an air of command over his warriors. Fierce determination burned in his onyx eyes, life I hadn't seen in him in too long. He may be a lot of things, but right now, Pollux was everything an Alpha should be.

He was the Alpha, the leader of our pack, and it was my duty to stand by his side, to fight alongside him in this battle against the hunters who sought to eradicate our kind. Eradicate everyone and anyone in order to get to Taylor. Even if he and I weren't on the best of grounds. This was my family's home, and I wouldn't allow it to fall.

As the wind blew through the trees, carrying whispers of unseen threats, I couldn't shake the guilt that gnawed at my conscience. It ate away at me, a relentless reminder of the cruel words I had hurled at her—Taylor, my charge who I had sworn to bring back to Asgard safely. A woman I was slowly falling for even though I shouldn't have been.

"They're out there somewhere. I can feel it," Pollux replied, his warriors waiting patiently, guarding the pack lands.

"I can't sense it like I used to."

It was true. Since I had become a guardian of Asgard and given up who I really was, I couldn't sense the danger like the others did. Shit, I didn't even have a wolf anymore. A part of me I gave up for the life I have now. A life that was forced by choice the night that my mother died. Pollux had asked me if I was ready to die for this, and back then I didn't know what I was signing myself up for.

Until Silas led me to the Phoenix temple, and I drank from a red vile that killed my wolf and let Cassie bring me back from death as an immortal warrior of the realms.

A guardian of the Arcane Gateway.

"I know, brother. Hopefully, we can handle this easily."

"You know that won't happen," I scoffed, rolling my eyes. "They won't stop till everyone is dead. But I guess it is good you have a guardian by your side."

My reply caused him to glance at me with a small smirk before he rolled his eyes. "You mean until they get what they want. You being a guardian or not."

"Eh, schematics," I replied with sarcasm as if I wasn't bothered. Even though deep down, I really was. I wasn't worried for myself, but I was worried for this pack.

The innocent people who were going to die.

He was referring to Taylor, but I knew damn well he wouldn't give her up. She was his ticket back to his family and if anything went wrong with that, he wouldn't ever forgive me or anyone else.

Looking back towards the pack house, I spotted the frame of her body staring out the dimly lit window. She was a sight to behold, and everything I had always hoped for in a woman. The time we had spent together was more than I could have ever asked for and yet I had treated her the way I did.

I was a complete asshole to her about her phone, and the way I yelled at her without listening was killing me. A part of me wanted to go speak to her right now, but I couldn't. I had to stay focused, and after I would fix things with her.

Amidst the chaos that seemed to follow us, I found solace in her presence, a respite from the weight of responsibility. But in a moment of blind anger, I had lashed out, pushing her away, desperate to shield her from the shit that was slowly approaching us.

It wasn't that I didn't think she was capable of handling herself. I knew she was capable, resilient even. Yet, in my misguided attempt to protect her, I had wounded her. I saw it in her eyes, the pain and disappointment in the way I had spoken to her.

However, that was just going to have to be something I tried to fix later.

If I even could.

For now, I had to push my guilt aside, to focus on the task at hand. The hunters were relentless, driven by a misplaced sense of duty to eradicate anything that they didn't deem normal by their own definition. An undoubtedly enticed by Moria, the woman who had taken Taylor and tried to raise her as her own.

The woman wasn't going to let Taylor go without a fight, and the fact she had made a pact with the hunters—the same ones who had killed so many of her kind—there was obviously nothing she wouldn't do.

"Where's Kara?" Pollux asked, a wave of uneasiness seemed to flow over him.

"At the house, guarding Taylor. Why?"

"Because they're here," he replied with venom laced in his words.

As the howls of border warriors echoed in the distance, I knew the hunters had made their way across our borders. The sounds of guns echoing in the distance as they attempted to take down their prey.

"The time is now!" Pollux yelled as the sounds of bones breaking echoed around me. A shift taking over him as he transformed into the massive wolf that I had seen him become so many times before. The beast snarling and pawing at the ground towards the treeline, my eyes turning to finally take in the figures of our enemies.

The hunters moved with lethal precision, their weapons glinting ominously in the soft light of the moon. No matter the situation, I was never going to allow them to get to Taylor. Never would I allow them to take what I fought so hard to obtain.

The clash of fangs and claws filled the air, mingled with the cries of pain and the thunderous beats of paws against the earth. The forest became a battleground, a tapestry of violence and defiance. I may not have been a shifter anymore, but I was skilled with hand to hand combat, and a sword was my calling.

Among other magical attributes.

If they wanted a battle, then I was going to fucking give them one.

CHAPTER
TWENTY-FOUR

<u>**Taylor**</u>

From the confines of the pack house, I watched as the battleground unfolded before me. Moonlight cast an ethereal glow upon the pack lawn, illuminating the fierce clash of beasts and armed hunters in a deadly dance of teeth, claws and guns. The constant echoed sound of one the hunters weapons going off filled my ears, bringing anguish and fury to my heart.

I never meant for any of this to happen, and the fact that the battle being my fault only made things hurt worse. People would lose their lives tonight, and all of it was because both sides wanted control of me.

Staring down amongst the chaos, blood scattered upon the ground—I spotted him. Tatum moved through the hunters like a skilled dancer through the crowd. His long silver blade sparkled under the moonlight as he slashed through all those who opposed him.

"It isn't too late to fix things."

Kara's voice came in loud and clear behind me. My head hung as I turned slowly to face her. "Are you here to tell me I'm stupid too?"

Again, with her quizzical look she laughed. "No, I shouldn't have to tell you that. You should already know it."

Ouch, really? Fucking bitch. That was like two times in a night.

"That's a little uncalled for," I replied with snark as I crossed my arms over my chest.

"Well, why don't you start listening to me and then maybe you may find the clarity you need," she replied. Her eyes narrowed at me like a mother scolding her child.

"Okay," I said through gritted teeth. "What do you suggest I do then?"

As her scolding look softened, the corner of her lips perked up into a small smirk as she glanced towards the window. "Why don't you start by seeking the enemy, that's lurking outside within the treelines."

Confused, I closed my mouth and turned to gaze out the window once more. My eyes searched for what she was talking about until my gaze settled upon a portion of treeline that in fact, gave me the clarity she was speaking of. There amongst the shadowed canopies were a group of people watching the battle unfold. I didn't recognize all of them, but there was one face I would never forget.

Moria—the woman who was supposed to be my mother.

Her being here confirmed what they were saying. She was working with the hunters, and because I could see their clear unity, it made me wonder if everything I had learned about my past so far had been accurate. Maybe she did kidnap me, take advantage of my scattered mind and used me to her own advantage.

A storm brewed within me, fueled by the constant stream of lies that had shrouded my true identity. How long had they kept me in the dark, aware of the power coursing through my veins? The truth had been twisted, hidden beneath layers of deception. My heart, no longer able to bear the weight of their lies.

Clenching my fists at my side, the anger within me grew. It's fury burning like a wildfire through my veins, fueled by the injustice I had been subjected to. No matter how angry I got, there was a small voice in the back of my mind that kept me sane. The voice of my father that urged me to remember who I was, and to embrace the dormant magic within me.

A magic that I thought I didn't know how to tap into, but standing here now—my mind seemed to clear slowly.

"It's time to end this," I muttered, turning on my heels prepared to face my past. Prepared to right the wrongs that had been done to me, and seek vengeance on a life that should never have been tampered with.

And of course, like the ghost she seemed to be—Kara had left me to deal with my emotions on my own.

Which is exactly what I wanted.

I emerged from the pack house, the scent of blood and dirt filling my nostrils. The sound of those injured and dying echoed in my ears. No matter how much I wanted to help them, deep down I knew I couldn't. Instead, I hyper focused on one goal—my darling mother.

My target lay before me, a figure I had both feared and longed to confront.

Guided by a determination that bordered on madness. I made my way forth, her eyes finally connecting with mine in a look of shock and a smile that quickly began to fall. I wasn't sure what I looked like in her eyes right then, but I hoped she felt the same fear that I had felt for years.

All of the anger, betrayal, and fury I had kept dormant inside me pressed forward. The surge of madness flowing off me, a tingling across my skin that made my heart race faster. It was as if time itself had stood still for me as I made my way through the masses of wolves and humans. As if the sea itself had parted as I made my way through.

"You!" I all but growled as I narrowed my gaze. Just in time to see a man running towards me only to be thrown hundreds of feet away with the simple flick of my hand.

"Taylor—" she gasped, backing away slowly as the men next to her seemed frantic. "You have to stop, we're here to save you."

"Enough, Mother," I sneered in disgust, "I know who you really are...and I know what you really are to me."

Her shock quickly diminished as her brow narrowed with what seemed to be irritation at my comment. "So you finally figured it all out, did you?"

Steps from her was where I stopped, my skin alight with a new found power I never knew that I had. The feeling of it coursing through me made me feel alive and for a moment I almost let it distract me. Until she opened her mouth again.

"I guess I should have kept you chained up better."

"What did you say?!" I snapped. "Chained up? You have lied to me my entire life!"

Shrugging her shoulders in a very nonchalant way, she smirked. "Yeah, but I guess I didn't do a good enough job of it."

I didn't realize she was distracting me until two men, who approached from behind, were nearly on top of me. A sudden burst of energy pulsated from my body as I quickly spun and rocketed them away, only to find that when I looked back my mother was running.

"REALLY MORIA!" I screamed out into the treeline, "DO YOU THINK RUNNING IS GOING TO SAVE YOU FROM ME!"

A primal roar escaped my lips as I lunged forward, propelled by fury and justice. My legs took me as fast as I could go as I chased after her through the forest, over broken branches and through the trees. She had underestimated me, underestimated the depths of my strength and resolve.

Something that would inevitably grant her the fate she deserved.

By the time I broke through the clearing of a small grove within the forest, I saw her still running at least ten yards ahead of me. My anger took control as I screamed into the air, throwing the energy built within my tiny frame directly at her. The power like a blue light surging towards her body knocking her to the ground.

The cry that escaped her didn't touch a single part of me as I slowed my pursuit, walking towards her figure that laid upon the ground. A desire for revenge and a thirst for blood I didn't even recognize. "Enough, Moira."

She quickly rolled over, scorched skin patches across her arms and chest. The blue shirt she had been wearing tattered in certain areas and black smudged markings on her face and neck. Almost as if the energy I hit her with had burned areas of her skin leaving a soot like residue behind.

"Taylor, please. I'm your mother—" she gasped out, clenching her stomach as she laid upon the ground. "They're lying to you."

"The only person who has been lying to me is you. How can you play innocent after what you said? After making a pact with the same hunters you tried to make me fearful of?"

Her lips parted, silence flowing as she stared at me dumbfounded.

"Just tell me why, Moria," I finally asked, wanting answers to the only question that had been bothering me since all of this began. "Why?"

She was quiet, her eyes darting towards the treeline as if she was hoping someone would come to her aid. However, after a moment, she realized that it was just the two of us and finally gave in to what I wanted to know.

"I was trying to keep you safe."

"Safe?!" I gasped, laughter escaping me as I shook my head. "In what world are you trying to keep me safe! You were using me to increase your own power."

Her eyes widened in shock before narrowing them. A hatred burned inside me as I immediately knew that it was true. She hadn't expected me to know that, but now that I did, what was keeping her from denying it further?

Her expression told me everything I needed to know.

"You're an ungrateful brat," she started to say before I jutted down, straddling her waist as I gripped her throat, prepared to watch life leave her eyes as she took her last breath.

"I'm a lot of things, but being ungrateful has never been one of them."

I wasn't sure exactly what was coming over me, but something deep inside me whispered in the back of my mind telling me her time had come to an end. That her life was no longer needed, and it was mine to claim.

"Taylor!" Tatum's voice called from somewhere out behind me, its warm melody wrapping around me as it once had but not touching me completely as the hatred I had for the woman I thought was my mother took precedence.

"Looks—like–you have–an audience—" she gasped out, my grip tightening.

"Taylor, stop. You can't kill her."

The sound of his footsteps coming to rest behind me halted me slightly, my eyes softening a little bit before narrowing in anger once more. "She took years of my life from me. She was only using me for her own personal gain."

"You don't know that," he replied, his deep musky scent wrapping around me as he stepped closer. "There are still so many things we need to find out from her. We can't have her die just yet."

He may have thought that, but I knew the truth. Because when I decided to take back my life, glimpses of my past had started to surface. Conversations that I hadn't remembered, and places that didn't seem familiar.

This girl is going to be everything to our reign...

Moria's voice rang loud and clear through the dark foggy depths of my mind.

Mother, you can't be serious. They are never going to let us keep her! My sister's voice etched with concern replied.

I don't care what they want. I'll have her convinced that we are the only family she can trust. She will do anything for me by the time I'm done with her.

As the small memory faded away, I realized that Tatum was calling my name again. Moria's eyes were wide as I continued to choke her. The only thing she cared about was power, and the power she had, the power she constantly tried to steal from me to restore herself, was the only thing keeping her alive.

"You don't deserve what I gave you..." I muttered, loosening my grip. A look of confusion passed her eyes as a smile crept across my face. "So I'm taking it back, all of it."

Letting my hand slide up to her jaw, I gripped it firmly as the other hand laid up on her forehead. She thrashed beneath me, eyes wide with fear. I didn't have a clue what I was doing, but the situation seemed right and without warning I leaned in close to her. "I hope you feel pain. Just like the pain you put in me."

Closing my eyes, I called to the power within her, my mind imagining the way it flowed to me. My body, calling it home.

A shiver of anticipation ran through me as I extended my hands, my palms hovering just above her thrashing body. The air crackled with an otherworldly energy as if the very fabric of reality trembled at the threshold of my power. I wanted everything she had, and everything she had stolen from me.

With a deep breath, I channeled a darkness deep inside. A darkness that softly called out to the woman's powers, a tantalizing allure that I couldn't resist. The desire to consume what she had was a hunger I had never experienced before. It was a delicate balance between control and surrender and I held the upper hand.

As my fingertips made contact with her skin, an electric surge coursed through my veins. I could feel the essence of her power, a pulsating force that sat silent waiting for me to take it.

Slowly opening my eyes I watched the glow that sparked out from my hands. The energy of her stolen powers cascaded through my fingertips, my body like a siphon taking everything she had. With each passing moment, I could feel my own powers growing, expanding to encompass the stolen energy.

And with every bit that flowed into me, the more I began to remember. Images and people flashing within my mind like a raging river, causing a gasp to escape my lips.

"Taylor, you have to stop! It's too much!"

Tatum's hand came to rest on my shoulder, but the moment he touched me a surge of electricity sent him flying back as if I was the lightning from the sky taking control of everything around me, awakening dormant parts of myself that I had never known existed.

Until, Moria's body was finally a lifeless form beneath me.

I felt a mix of exhilaration and trepidation. The stolen power coursed through my veins, transforming me into something more than I had ever been. The path I had chosen had irrevocably changed me, and I had to tread carefully. After years feeling like I was in the dark, I finally could see the light.

I remembered almost everything, slowly things were coming in. Parts of me that I didn't know existed. I wasn't sure how long it would take me to gain control of my life, of who I was and what had happened to me but I wasn't going to let anyone control me again.

I wasn't going to lose sight of who I was a second time.

I rose from the lifeless body, a sense of clarity washed over me. The world seemed sharper, brighter, as if my perception had been heightened. Turning, I came face to face with Tatum, who stood staring at me with parted lips as if he wasn't sure what I was going to do next.

Tilting my head to the side, I watched him. "I'm not going to hurt you."

"I know," he nodded. "You killed her?"

The statement came out more as a question as I casually looked behind me for a second before turning back to him. "She deserved to die for her sins. She stole what didn't belong to her, and she stole from the wrong person."

"Taylor—"

"That's not my name," I quickly replied. The sound of the name had a sickening taste on my tongue that made my nose wrinkle in disgust. "Never address me like that again."

"Okay–" he replied slowly. "What do you want me to call you?"

Stepping forward, I made my way towards him, surprised that he stood his ground as I approached. "My name is Brina."

"Tay–" I glared at him as he cleared his throat. "I mean Brina. I—"

Holding my hand up, I shook my head. "It doesn't matter, Tatum. The battle is done. We need to return."

Even though I remembered who I was, it hurt for me to speak to him. I was still the same person, I was simply finally awake. I hated being dismissive with him. I wanted more than anything for him to wrap me up in his arms and kiss me, but he made it clear before he had more important things to do.

I wasn't sure if he regretted what had happened between us, but I wasn't going to make the mistake of being a fool again.

Instead, I had to get back the life that was wrongfully taken from me.

CHAPTER TWENTY-FIVE

Stepping through the clearing of the forest, the blood-soaked battleground sat before me. The aftermath of the harrowing clash between the hunters and Pollux's pack had come to an end. The scent of death hung heavy in the air, mingling with the cries of the wounded, who were slowly being tended to. My heart hung heavy at the view before me.

None of this was what I wanted.

Everywhere I turned, shifters were moving towards the wounded, trying to help in any way that they could. Women, searching for their husbands and the mournful cries of those who lost the ones they loved. The guilt over it all threatened to consume me, but I couldn't allow it.

It wasn't my fault, no matter what anyone may think.

"You!" a deep hearty voice bellowed out, causing me to spin around, coming face to face with Pollux, an angry Alpha who seemed to be on a mission. "You stupid fucking girl! Do you see what you have done?!"

"What?" I gasped. My eyes searched around the area, taking in the many narrowed gazes of the wolves who were watching our interaction. "This isn't my fault."

"All of this is your fault!" he snapped, his arms open wide as he gestured around at the devastation. "All because you wanted to be stubborn and foolish with what we were trying to do to help you."

Anger coursed through my veins, fueled by the knowledge that they had played a part in the tragedy that unfolded. Yet, here he stood, trying to place all the blame on me as if he was innocent in everything. As if he wasn't the one who had been searching for me for years to help his own needs.

As if he hadn't already known that the hunters had always been chasing after me.

"You dare to blame me?" I spat, my voice laced with fury as I approached the Alpha, my once-submissive demeanor replaced by a newfound strength. "You and your brother, with your web of deceit, have brought this upon us all!"

Pollux's eyes narrowed, his voice thick with defiance as he refused to acknowledge what I was saying. "You were the catalyst, the one who attracted the hunters with your mere existence. This could have been avoided if you had only known your place."

My place?

A bitter laugh escaped my lips as I crossed my arms over my chest. My eyes glanced around once more until they fell on Tatum, who stepped towards me, shaking his head. "Don't. Brina, please."

"Brina?" Pollux scoffed in a mocking tone as he said my name. "What...she changed her fucking name?"

"For a man who is an Alpha, you surely are conceited and ignorant about many things," I replied, raising a brow as if to question who he was.

He lunged forward, stopped in his tracks by Tatum, who tried to help prevent the altercation that Pollux surely wanted. I knew that his wolf was on edge, an Alpha who had lost so many of his pack members. I had heard stories from Logan about how agonizing the pain of losing them can be.

Though I didn't imagine ever being in a position to see it myself.

"You need to learn to respect the hand that feeds you." He snarled, his eyes darkening over, catching me slightly off guard. I was trying desperately to rein myself in. To control the magic flowing through me, but Pollux was making it hard for me to let go because of how he was addressing me.

"The hand that feeds me?" I replied mockingly.

"Brina, don't." Tatum quickly replied, his eyes begging me to not continue whatever it was that I was going to say.

At one point in my life, I would have cowered at this show of dominance. Granted, I was a defiant character myself before. But now I was slowly realizing who and what I was and though I didn't have every piece, I knew I wouldn't tolerate this.

"You dare to speak of my place when you and your brother have lied to me from the beginning? When you have hidden the full truth of who I am and the dangers that surround us? You're the Alpha of this pack Pollux, and you didn't even tell them what you were doing. So instead of directing your anger at me, perhaps you should be tending to your wounded. The battle is over."

"You fucking bitch!"

Moving quickly, he lunged past Tatum, who tried to grab him. His anger directed at me as he moved towards me. It wasn't clear what he thought he was going to do, but the last thing I would let him do was touch me.

The moment he stepped within two feet of my body, his proud stature crumbled to the ground, a power unrecognizable forcing him to his knees before me. Eyes wide and mouth open, I could see the fear dancing within his eyes, mirroring the vulnerability I had felt for far too long.

"Did you actually think that you could hurt me?" I seethed, my voice commanding and unwavering. "You and your brother may have brought me here for your own purposes, but I will not be subjected to ill treatment because you're angry. Don't forget that the two of you are the reason for me being here. The two of you are the ones who lied to me and only slowly revealed information when you thought it was beneficial for me to know something. I know the truth now, Pollux. I remember what had been taken from me so long ago, and I will not be silenced any longer."

Tatum, once filled with bravado, took a hesitant step back, watching me with uncertainty that only made the pain in my heart hurt even worse. "We only wanted to protect you, to keep you safe."

"Protect me?" I scoffed, the bitterness of betrayal weighing heavily upon me. "By keeping me in the dark? By trying to get to my heart in order to make me trust you more?"

I knew that Pollux wouldn't understand what I was talking about, but Tatum did. The message was loud and clear in the air with him as his eyes widened slightly in shock. I slept with him, and had allowed myself to feel something for him. Only to realize that it was just part of their act.

As much as I had hoped that what had happened between us could have been real, I would only be lying to myself.

As I spoke, memories flooded back, fragments of my past weaving together to form a tapestry of truth. Balder was indeed my father, and I was no normal creature. Hell, I wasn't even a succubus at all. I was a goddess, a siphon that had the power to take and give life where I needed to.

But tonight, my presence had caused me to be the reaper of death.

I was the Hallow.

An Elder god, who served Fate when he needed me.

"The time has come for me to return home where I belong," I declared, my voice carrying the weight of the pain I felt. "I have been gone for far too long, and the only way that people will be safe in this realm...is for me to return home."

Slowly, I released Pollux from the command of my powers. His body fell forward on the ground as he panted, catching his breath. A twinge of guilt filled me as I took in the confused expressions of his pack members. It wasn't typical that an Alpha would be put in the position he was in, and I had compromised his position by doing what I did.

As much as I wanted to let him suffer in that situation, I couldn't.

"Pollux is your Alpha and tonight he will lead you through victory, no matter how this terrible battle was caused. I'm proud to know that he is here to lead your pack, and one day...his son will take his place to lead you further into victory."

My eyes scanned the masses as I spoke. Seeking out anyone who would object to what I was about to ask, because regardless of our differences, I knew this pack was important. I wasn't sure how I knew, but deep down I did. This family's reign could not be impacted by what happened here.

"Does anyone here object to what I'm saying?" I finally asked, as my eyes landed on Pollux once more, who had slowly stood to his feet, glaring at me. "Is there anyone here who objects to my words of loyalty to your Alpha?"

Silence filled the air with my question. Until one by one, each wolf that had been standing dropped to their knees, bowing to Pollux out of respect. A sign that hopefully would show him that I was on his side, even if he had been a complete fucking asshole.

"Good," I replied calmly as I turned my attention to the man who brought me here. I was still angry at him. The sense of betrayal lingered in my core as I tried to push it away. After all, there was no reason anymore to continue the charade. "Tatum?"

His eyes quickly met mine as a small smile appeared across his lips. Lips that less than twenty-four hours ago, I wanted nothing more than to kiss. However, now that notion seemed so far away. "Yeah?"

"It's time for us to leave."

CHAPTER

TWENTY-SIX

When I told Tatum that I was ready to go, I hadn't expected everything to happen so quickly, but honestly... I wasn't sure why I thought that way. However, as the pack took care of their own, I had made my way back to the pack house only to find myself beneath the hot water of my bathroom shower. The steam filled the room as the water cascaded down around me.

I had held myself together as well as I could out there in front of everyone, but the moment that I found myself alone, I crumbled. The tears, unable to stop flowing, tried to piece together everything that had ever happened to me. The pain of the memories that slowly flooded in, mixed with that of the ones I had after my memory had been taken.

None of this was supposed to happen this way. And knowing that so many people died just because I existed killed me.

All I wanted was to be normal. To live a normal life. To go back to my shop in Salem and act like all of this had just been a bad dream.

But I couldn't.

That notion was just a delusional fantasy of a woman who wasn't ready to take back the responsibilities she had been given thousands of years ago.

Turning off the water of the shower, the heat flooding away down the drain, I stepped out wrapping a towel around me as I tried to let go of what I was feeling to prepare myself for the shitstorm that was coming.

I didn't have the slightest clue as to what I was going to be walking into stepping foot back in Asgard. I didn't feel exactly like that was the place I belonged to, but I felt I had to go there. As if that place was calling to me, and something important was waiting for me to arrive.

Slipping on my clothing, I ran a brush through my hair as I stared at myself in the mirror. I didn't look any different than I had before, but I felt like I was completely brand new. As if my entire existence had changed, and my life was no longer my own.

"Brina?" The name sounded so foreign on my lips, but I knew that's who I was. I wasn't Taylor like I had thought for so many years. I was Brina, the daughter of Fate and bringer of life and death.

"Brina?" My name being said again caused me to sigh. I turned towards the bedroom door, knowing fully well that it was Tatum on the other side who had called my name twice. I didn't want to speak to him yet, nor did I want to see his face.

But I was going to have to. I couldn't avoid him for long, and he was my guardian to the other side. A guardian my father Balder had told me to trust.

Even if I thought that notion was questionable.

"You can come in," I finally replied, my voice barely above a whisper as I felt the weight of my guilt and sadness pressing down on me.

Slowly, the door opened. Tatum stood there looking every part of the sex god he was, hair dripping wet obviously fresh from the shower. "I just wanted to see if you were ready to go?"

Nodding, I gave myself one more look in the mirror before turning back to him. "Yeah, I'm ready."

"Look, before we go, I was hoping we could talk."

My eyes lifted to meet him as I frowned. "About what?"

"About us..." he replied, but I shook my head, not wanting to touch on that topic whatsoever.

"There is nothing to talk about, Tatum. It was very clear that you don't want a repeat of that, and don't worry, I won't tell anyone."

"What?" he gasped, mouth wide as a mixture of a scoff and laugh escaped his lips. "That's not at all what I was going to say—wait, do you regret what happened between us?"

Of course, I hadn't regretted what happened. I loved every moment of it, and I wanted more. I had a hard time being within a few feet of him without the memories of our time together flooding through my mind. My body going through the motions of the way he touched me and how he made me feel.

I wanted more, so much more.

But I knew that couldn't happen. He and I could never be together, and the moment we got back, he would be free of me. So why hurt myself even further.

Clearing my throat I shook my head. "No, but let's face it...I'm your charge until we get back to Asgard. Once I'm there, you will be free to live your life again while I have work to do. There is no point of making our situation even more difficult than it already is."

He stared at me with a blank expression before shaking his head, turning towards the door. "Yeah, I guess you're right. I will be free, won't I?"

I hadn't expected his words to hurt me like they did, but the ache was like a knife to my heart. "Shall we get going then?" I tried to say as steadily as possible. Hoping he wouldn't see how much his reply had affected me.

"Yeah, let's go."

Standing before the portal, my heart pounded within my chest. A mixture of trepidation and anticipation filled me as I prepared to leave this world for the next. Even though I had probably done this more than a million times, I didn't remember it like that. I didn't have any memory of going to other realms or walking through portals.

Which I didn't even know was how we made our way to where we were going.

The portal shimmered with an otherworldly cerulean glow, beckoning me to step through and leave behind the only life I could really remember. This world had been my home for as long as I could remember, but it was no longer where I truly belonged. The memories of my past were foggy, veiled by a mysterious amnesia caused by a woman who only cared for her own greed then that of the people around her.

But now, as I prepared to step forward into my new life, I could feel the pull of my true origins tugging at my soul. A tug that called me home.

"Are you ready to go home, Brina?"

Kara's voice echoed behind me. However, this time I didn't turn to face her. I actually knew very well who she was now, and as the memories slowly trickled in I realized how I knew her.

She was an old friend, a wise woman I had always been able to speak my mind to.

Images of days where we had spent time in my home in the Hallow reflected in my mind as we discussed things over drinks and stayed up late speaking about different people. But most of all, I remembered the day she came to me and asked me to save a man on earth, a Sølvmane who needed to be kept alive in order to make sure my father's sights stayed true.

"You should already know by now, Kara, that I'm always ready."

She chuckled as she stepped beside me. "I'm happy to have you back, old friend."

As I glanced at her, I smiled. "I'm not fully back yet, and honestly, this time feels different. As if I'm here, but I'm not."

"Yes, I figured that might happen. Finnick will be able to assist with that, though."

"Finnick?" I questioned the name unfamiliar on my lips.

"Yes," she replied. "Let's get you back and we can talk more there."

Taking a deep breath, I gathered all the courage I could manage and took the first step into the shimmering light with Tatum and Kara. The world around me dissolved into a white fog-like color as if I was floating within the clouds, yet walking across hard ground. I didn't have the slightest clue as to what I was doing or where I was going, but looking towards Tatum—he seemed unfazed. So I followed.

Eventually, the cloud-like fog lifted and bright green grass emerged on the other side. Tall white pillars surrounded me, a courtyard of flowers and scents that overpowered the senses in a good way. Everything here was so much brighter, so much more alive than what I was accustomed to on earth.

"I'm definitely not in Kansas anymore," I muttered to myself, only for Tatum to scoff at my comment.

"You weren't, you were in Idaho. Now you're in Asgard."

Annoyed by his comment, I wasn't going to let his attitude ruin this moment for me. "Right."

Clearing her throat, Kara stepped forward as she looked between Tatum and I. "Enough with the attitude, both of you. It's starting to annoy me."

Choosing to ignore what she said, I spun around slowly as I took in everything with the courtyard, from the vines that grew on everything to the bright purple and pink colors of the sky.

"This is amazing," I gasped, a smile spread wide across my face.

"Yeah, well let's get going. You can admire things later. I need to take you to meet someone," Tatum replied, as he made his way towards the massive white marbled building that sat to the left of me.

He took the steps two and a time, causing me to run to quickly catch up to him. No matter the memories that I had felt on earth, nothing was coming back to me here. This place was all new to me, and because of that, I didn't want to get lost.

Catching up to him, I fell in step behind him as we walked down the grand halls of the building. Everything was white everywhere you looked, and it was clear that whoever owned this place wasn't one for decorating.

Yet, as we turned the corner to head down another hall, music began to fill my ears until we came to a massive set of double doors.

Stopping in his tracks, Tatum sighed, and turned to gaze at me from over his shoulder. "Whatever you do, stay by my side until we get to the front of the hall. There are going to be multiple people who want to speak to you, but you can't until we see who we have come to see."

"Okay," I replied slowly, slightly hesitant and confused, but it was clear he knew more than I did at this moment so who was I to disagree.

The double doors opened, and I was blown away. The grand hall was adorned with opulent decorations of gold accents, white walls, and diamond-like fixtures. But most importantly, it was filled with people dressed in vibrant colored clothing, from fancy dresses to more relaxed modern day designs.

The entire place was a sight beyond imagination, and the air was thick with magic, an ethereal energy that hummed within the atmosphere, wrapping around me gently as I stepped in as if to greet me home.

As I navigated through the hall, marveling at the tapestries that adorned the walls and the ornate chandeliers hanging from the ceiling, I sensed the presence of someone important. Though I didn't spot her until Tatum came to a stop in front of a mass that slowly parted way for us, allowing my gaze to fall upon a woman, regal and commanding.

Long fuchsia colored hair hung in soft waves down over her shoulder towards her waist. Her eyes were a mesmerizing star-like blue that seemed to see the universe without her ever leaving the room. The moment that her eyes met mine, I could sense an unspoken connection as if our fates were intricately intertwined.

A familiarity that seemed to spark in her own gaze as her smile began to grow.

"Brina," she said softly as she stood to her feet, making her way down the white marbled steps towards me. The two men who stood beside her watched her every move. One, a dark-haired man with a five o'clock shadow that had a look upon his face as if he hated the world, and the other a man with golden red eyes who raised a brow and then gestured Tatum to come closer.

However, none of it mattered in the moment when the woman approached me. Her arms quickly wrapped around me as she pulled me closer. "Welcome home," she whispered into my ear before pulling away. "I know you don't remember me, but I feel like I have known you for a lifetime. I'm Cassie, the heir to Asgard."

Shit...what do I do now? Do I bow? Oh wait, maybe it's curtsey. Fuck what do I do?

Taking a moment to catch my breath, I tried to determine what it was I was supposed to do and simply settled for bowing. However, the moment I did snickering came from a few people around and I found myself embarrassed and confused as to what I had done wrong.

Cassie, though, didn't find anything funny and quickly turned to them with a glare that made them flee and turn their heads.

"I'm sorry, did I do something wrong?" I piped up, slightly confused.

Her eyes met mine again as she chuckled softly and shook her head. "No, not at all. However, you're royalty as well. You don't have to bow to me. Technically, on earth we would be considered family. But not like blood related or anything because that would be weird as hell seeing as you slept with my brother."

What?!

I internally felt myself fall out. One, how the fuck did she know that and two, what the hell did she mean we were family?! Like siblings? Or cousins? Or like a marriage thing?

My mind was going a mile a minute, and she must have realized because the laughter that left her as she placed a gentle hand on my arm made my stomach turn.

"Oh, calm down," she said in a teasing manner. "I promise you it's nothing bad like what you must be thinking. Now, come one. We have much to talk about."

I wasn't sure what the hell she wanted to discuss with me, but if it was anything like what she said just a second ago...I wasn't sure I could handle that kind of excitement.

CHAPTER
TWENTY-SEVEN

<u>Tatum</u>

Watching my sister walk away with Brina had been hard. I hadn't anticipated us coming here to have gone the way it had, but there was nothing I could do to really change it. She had made her choice back on Earth when it came to what had happened between us, and I was in no place to question her.

She was a goddess, and I was simply a guardian.

"Tate, are you listening to me?" Silas asked, causing me to turn my attention to him once more. He glanced between me and where the girls had gone and then back to me with a look of concern. "Is there something I should know?"

"No," I replied with confidence, trying to keep my face completely void of emotion.

Silas had been ruling at my sister's side for years now. When Finnick—once the prince of the Fae realm, now the King—won the Asgardian games for Cassie's hand, Silas took up ruling in Asgard while Finnick returned home. At first, many questioned the choice, and there were numerous who tried to oppose it. However, Odin made it clear that the opposition wouldn't be allowed, and those who wouldn't obey fled for other places.

It had been years since the issues arose and within those years my sister and her mates found happiness in their lives together. Though she couldn't be with all of them when she wanted to, she made it work the best she could.

And in return, gave birth to the children of Asgard.

Orym, the eldest and son of Finnick. The next ruler of Tver. Then twins Ayla and Erren, the daughter and son of Silas. Ayla, was a wicked little girl with a mischievous streak and Erren was a commanding future warrior having followed in his father's footsteps.

Cassie had thought she was done after the twins or so Silas had told us a hundred times, but of course, Faeryn, the princess of the Fae came shortly after. Her beauty was something that the Fae cherished, and as Finnick's pride and joy, she became the apple of her parent's eye.

"You seem to have a hard time following the conversation tonight," Silas said, pulling me from my thoughts once more as Lucas caught my attention, carrying a tiny little girl in his arms no older than two. Her black hair and bright blue eyes stood out against any crowd and the moment she spotted me she squealed with glee.

"I'm sorry, Silas. Just a bit worn out," I replied, trying to maintain the respect as I smiled at Della within her father's arms. "Hello princess, did you miss me?"

Out of all of my sister's children, Della was my favorite. I wasn't sure of the connection I had with her, but it was as if we were kindred spirits. Connected by more than just blood. "I don't know what her fascination with you is, Tate. The nurse maid called me to come collect her because she just wouldn't settle."

"Well, Della is going to have to wait," Silas piped up, an irritated look upon his face as he let out a heavy breath and slowly stood to his feet. "We have a lot to discuss. Once we're done, you can do what you want."

I wasn't one to object to my brother-in-law's words. If my sister was here, I knew for fact she would tell Silas to leave me alone until tomorrow, but I was glad to get this over with now. It would mean that my job was finally completed, and I would be free to do whatever it is that I wanted.

Which is exactly what I needed right now.

Time to breathe and rest after years of searching for Brina.

Watching Silas step down off the throne area, I followed behind him out the side door towards his office. I had been there many times, and this time I knew I would be like the others. The only difference was that there wasn't a mission after this one.

I had been promised that this would be the last task I would have to do for a while.

That bringing Brina here would grant me a long time for reprieve. However, I was suddenly questioning if I wanted that. Being around her and not being able to love her the way I so desperately wanted was an agonizing thought.

Stepping into the office, I closed the door behind Silas and I watched as Silas took a seat behind the dark wood desk that sat in the center of the room.

"Now that we don't have any distractions. Shall we start from the top?"

Nodding my head, I took a seat in the chair he gestured towards. "Of course."

"Great," he replied with a smile. "So tell me, where did you find her?"

"Salem, Massachusetts, like you suggested. She was living a somewhat mundane life. I found her in an alley. I thought she was having a run in with a shifter, but she was the one who had gotten the upper hand. From there we talked at her apartment, but she attempted to run. We were finally able to get on some normal ground at a cabin she owned in the woods a few hours from Salem."

Silas listened intently, nodding his head here and there as I explained to him about the run in with the hunters in the woods, and the rest of the journey up until we got to the pack lands. However, one thing I did leave out was the intimate moments between Brina and I.

I should have told him, but there was no way that I was going to share that information with anyone. I would cherish them even if she didn't.

"Oh, and she isn't Taylor anymore. Now that she re-members who she is, she wants to be called by her real name—Brina."

"Oh really?" he repeated, gazing up at me with a raised brow. "I'm surprised she didn't keep the other name. I kind of liked the thought of calling her Taylor."

"Why?"

He shrugged for a moment, as if pondering over an old memory before he cleared his throat. "It doesn't matter. What matters now is that we have her here. Now we have to work towards securing the future."

I didn't know in full detail what 'securing the future' meant, but I had a feeling it had to do with a few of the future children having power issues that had grown uncontrollable over the years. Especially Pandora and Faeryn.

"I'm happy to have assisted Asgard," I finally replied, wait-ing for him to dismiss me.

However, instead, he sat quietly. Staring at me as if he want-ed to say something in regards to our meeting but as if he was unsure of how to ask it. Silas and I had never been close. Our relationship had always been purely business, and because of that we didn't pry into each other's lives.

"You may be excused if you would like," he finally muttered, gesturing towards the door as he picked up a pen writing things down on a piece of paper upon his desk.

"Thank you." He didn't have to tell me twice, making my way towards the door.

"Oh and, Tate."

Stopping in my tracks, my hand on the door knob I sighed and glanced over my shoulder at him. "Yes?"

"Please make sure that she is ready to leave for Tver the day after tomorrow. Finnick is waiting for her arrival, and will continue to help her recover there."

"Wait, what? She isn't staying in Asgard?" Questioning Silas was completely out of my character. His eyes slowly lifted from what he was doing to meet my gaze with a look of curiosity.

"Yes, Tate. She is needed in Tver. Is there a problem?"

I shook my head, not wanting to have to explain to Silas why I cared. It wasn't like my feelings actually mattered on this anyways. "No problem. Just glad to have the mission over."

Silas chuckled as if to find amusement in what I said, but there was still a glint of hesitation and curiosity in his eyes that made me wonder if he believed a word I said.

"Alright then, go enjoy yourself. I have a few things to settle here, and I will be off to find my lovely wife."

Internally cringing, I could have done without that bit of information and left as quickly as I could. The moment the door closed behind me though, I found the weight of everything that had transpired sinking in. Silas and Cassie were planning on sending Taylor—or Brina—as she said, away.

My thoughts of a normal happy life with a woman slowly fading into the dark void.

Taylor

Settling into the plush light-blue armchair in Cassie's room, I took in the grand splendor of the apartment-like suite around me. The decor spoke of royalty and sophistication, with gilded accents and rich fabrics adorning every surface. The soft glow of candlelight flickered, casting an ethereal ambiance over the room. It was so different from the way I had lived back on earth, and to see that people here in this place lived like this... it took me away.

It was like something out of a fairytale, and the mix of modern and old traditions were everywhere you looked. Holding the crystal stemmed wine glass in my hand that a servant had offered me the moment I walked in the room, I pondered what it was that Cassie had whisked me away for. The crimson liquid within the cup swirling slightly as I lifted the glass to my lips savoring the velvety liquid inside.

Cassie sat across from me on a small white settee, her eyes concentrated on me as if she was deep in thought. Yet there was a smile on her face, and a familiarity in her gaze that spoke of warmth and a long-standing connection we must have had.

Though I couldn't quite remember it.

I still didn't understand how it was possible to have known someone your entire life, and not remember a single memory at the same time.

"Cassie," I began cautiously, breaking the comfortable silence that had settled between us, "I want to thank you for having me here. But I do want to let you know that... I don't remember you or anything about this place."

Cassie's smile faltered for a moment, her eyes filled with a mix of sympathy and determination. "I know. It's to be expected though, after everything you have gone through. As for this place—" she gestured to the room around us as if to gesture to Asgard in general. "You never actually came here. I knew you in Tver.

Tver. The name echoed within me, stirring a distant resonance. It held a weight, a significance that I couldn't fully comprehend. Taking a deep breath I sat my glass down on the glass table nearby and leaned forward, resting my elbow on my knee as I stared at her.

"Why am I here, Cassie? Why is all of this happening?"

The excitement didn't quite return to Cassie's eyes that I had expected to see. Since I met her she seemed overwhelmed with joy in my presence. But there was something about my question that seemed to trouble her, instead.

"I actually need your help with something." She finally admitted as she sipped on her wine. "My niece, Pandora. She and my daughter Faeryn are in need of a guide—or mentor. Someone who can teach them how to gain control of their powers, and if they can't—someone who can take them away, only to give them back when it's time for them to have them."

Her truth stunned me. My eyes went wide, my lips parted as I slowly nodded my head, trying to wrap my mind around what she was saying.

"... and you think I can help you? I mean, don't get me wrong, I'm flattered that a goddess would trust me with something like this... with her child. But Cassie, I don't know anything about the power I have or about myself. I'm still getting my memories. I don't know how I can help you."

"I understand," she replied as a smile slowly spread across her soft pink lips. "I have been where you are right now, Brina. I have stood in your position trying to understand who I was, and what my position in life was. It's hard, I won't lie to you. But having someone at your side to catch you when you fall can help."

"...but I don't have anyone." I chuckled. "I don't have a mate or mates like you do."

Her eyes widened with mischievousness glint as a smirk peaked the corner of her mouth. "Oh… but don't you?"

Furrowing my brow, I tried to understand what she was getting at. "I'm pretty sure I don't. I think I would know."

Shrugging her shoulders, she relaxed back further into her seat as she rested her wrist on her knee, her glass hanging loosely within her hand. "You could have fooled me with how much sexual tension was coming of you and Tate."

Tatum.

Just the sound of his name made my heart ache. Yes, we had shared something, but it wasn't more than a one-time thing. "I think you're mistaking that situation, Cassie."

"Brina, my uncle of sorts—or your father, is the god of fate. He doesn't let anything happen by chance. There is a reason why your body betrays you when you speak about him."

My body? There was no way that my body was betraying me. I was clear minded about my decision. I made that final before I came to Asgard.

Raising a brow, she gave me a pointed look. "See, it's betraying you now as you think about what I said."

What the fuck? How does she know I'm thinking about him?

Clearing my throat, I forced a smile to my face before shaking my head. "No, honestly, you're mistaken. Even if I did want him, he doesn't want me. That was made clear."

Laughter erupted from Cassie as she watched me. "Brina, I have known Tate his entire life and even beyond. That man is crazy about you, but he is too proud to admit it."

"How would you know that?" I asked, softly. Confusion filling me.

"Let's just say that we both have our own unique gifts, Brina. As time goes on, you will be able to grow yours just as I have. Just know that if you went to him right now... you would be welcomed with open arms."

Speechless, I sat there, my heart filled with hope while my mind filled with fear and hesitation. Did I want to take that risk or would I pass it by and live a life-time of regret in not knowing if there could be something between us?

After a moment of consideration, I let my gaze fall to her once more.

"I suppose time will tell me what fate has in store."

Chapter
Twenty-Eight

Standing outside Tatum's door, my heart pounded in my chest. The hallway felt suffocating, the air heavy with anticipation. I had rehearsed the words I wanted to say a hundred times, each time hoping to find the courage to confront the man that had helped me recover who I was. A man who helped me to feel again. But now, as I stood on the precipice of truth, fear gripped me.

What if he rejected me?

What if he confirmed my worst fears?

The mere thought sent shivers down my spine. Our past conversations replayed in my mind, twisting my perception, leaving me confused about his true intentions. I had convinced myself that he wanted nothing to do with me, that I was merely a passing shadow in his life. However, no matter how many times I attempted to accept that fate, I couldn't.

There was something about him that I couldn't let go.

Something that had me begging for more.

After speaking with Cassie, her words unlocked a glimmer of hope. Hope that perhaps everything I had thought was true was actually wrong. Maybe I had missed something, maybe I had mistaken his silence or redirection for his own fear of rejection. Or perhaps I was simply a fucking fool about to make the biggest mistake of her life.

Either way, it was eating me alive, not knowing. I wasn't sure exactly what Cassie had in mind other than helping her daughter and her niece, and of course before I left her room, letting me know that I was going to the Fae kingdom. But I was willing to try and explore new paths.

I mean, hell, I'd be running from shit for as long as I could remember. So maybe it was time to start putting my faith in the right people, and seek a new path that could bring me closer to the person I used to be.

I stood outside his door, compelled to know the truth, no matter the cost.

"You can do this," I muttered with a heavy sigh. "Don't be a chicken shit."

Summoning every ounce of bravery, I raised my hand and knocked, the sound echoing through the silence. I hadn't known where to find him, but Cassie was more than happy to have her servant show me the way when I told her I would consider it. Almost as if she knew that I was going through with this crazy idea.

Or almost like she was hoping that he and I would make things work.

Seconds felt like an eternity as I waited, my breath caught in my throat. The door creaked open, and there he stood before me, a mixture of surprise and confusion etched across his face. Those same deep blue mesmerizing eyes staring down at me, captivating me the same way they had when I had seen him in my shop.

Everything about Tatum made me want more, and right now, shirtless-Tatum with shorts hanging low on his hips made a hunger start to bubble inside me I hadn't been expecting to be there. A desire and lust that I couldn't control no matter how much I wanted too.

For a moment, my mind went blank. My carefully prepared speech vanished into thin air. "Um, hi. I...I didn't expect you to answer." I stumbled over my words, my voice barely a whisper.

"You're knocking on my door, why wouldn't I answer?"

Shrugging my shoulders gingerly, I glanced around the hallway. "Right. Do you think we can talk?"

He raised a brow, crossing his arms over his chest as if calculating whether or not a conversation with me was what he wanted. "Is everything alright? Did something happen?"

"No." I sighed, shaking my head. "Nothing happened, I just wanted to talk to you about something...preferably not in the hallway."

He glanced around for a moment, the hallway empty but the silence almost eerie.

"If that's what you want," he replied softly, as he stepped aside, pushing the door open further so that I could pass him into the room. I noticed how similar it was in size to Cassie's. It was as if this place was its own apartment building. Dark walls met dark blankets upon a four-poster bed, accented with bits of silver and white.

The dark contrast of the room to Tatum's personality really surprised me. I hadn't taken him to be the type of man who had a room that reeked of gloom and despair, but then again, I had been wrong about him so far.

"So what's so important you needed to speak to me?" he asked, brushing past me as he made his way towards a cream-colored sofa in front of a currently lit fireplace. He flopped down onto the thick cushions as he relaxed back, his legs spread out in front of him slightly as his hands rested upon his thighs.

Panic filled me with his question. Yes, I had rehearsed what I was going to say, but now that the moment presented itself I was acting like a fool. My mind was completely blank when it came to the plan I was going to stick to.

"Uh, well...I wasn't sure about the customs of the Fae. I was going to ask you for pointers."

Lie. It was a complete and utter fucking lie...I may not have known what I said, but that wasn't why I was here.

Knitting his brow together, he frowned. "You're lying."

"Uh, no–no, I'm not."

He stared at me with what seemed like irritation until once again he stood to his feet, his tall well-built physique completely catching me off guard as he slowly made his way towards where I was standing. "Is that right? Sure there isn't anything else on your mind, Brina?"

Caught in my own web of lies, I took a deep breath, my voice steady but laced with vulnerability. "I think so?"

It wasn't what I wanted to say, but I couldn't even formulate my thoughts correctly to know where I was going with the lie. All I knew was that watching him walk towards me the way he was, I was a complete and utter fucking mess.

One step. Two steps. Until he was right in front of me.

My back unknowingly found its way towards the wall. The hard surface not allowing me to get any further from him that I already was. Which wasn't far considering he stood two feet in front of me, his arm raised as his palm met the wall by my head.

"Do you want to try again? Perhaps, with the truth, Brina."

Shit.

"Okay—okay," I gasped, my heart racing as I stared at him. "When I was talking to your sister, she told me that I was misreading everything with you. That—what happened between us may have meant more to you..."

A snort escaped him as he rolled his eyes. "Sounds to me like my sister needs to mind her own fucking business."

"Hey, she was just trying to give me advice. What's wrong with that?"

Shaking his head, he leaned back from where he had me caged, but continued to stare down at me from only two feet away. "My sister has a tendency to overthink things. I love her to death, but she can be nosey as hell when she wants something done her way."

"Oh."

It was the only thing I could think to say while I stood there feeling like a complete fool. I didn't know her like he did, and so I jumped at what she was saying. But perhaps I jumped too premature for this kind of situation. "I guess me being here was for nothing then."

"Why don't you tell me what nothing is and I can tell you if it was all for nothing."

This was it, it was now or never. I was going to tell him, and he was either going to laugh in my face or something else would happen. Whatever that may have been.

"She said that you want me just as bad as I want you..." I whispered, a heat of embarrassment rushing over my cheeks as I quickly made my way towards the door.

"...and where do you think you're going?" he asked, as he snatched me by the wrist, pushing me against the wall, only to cage me once more. "We're not done talking."

"Tatum…" I muttered, my breath catching in my throat. "What are you doing?"

A smirk slowly grew on the corner of his lips as he stared at me. Leaning close to me, his lips brushed against my jawline as he leaned in towards my ear. "I dream of you, Brina. My cock hardens at the mere thought of your naked body writhing underneath me. The idea of your lips wrapped around my dick makes me cum harder than I ever have before. Is that what you want to hear, Brina? That I have wanted you since the first time I laid eyes on you, and even if this conversation never happened, do you really think I would have let you go to the Fae realm without me? You're mine, Brina. Forever and Always."

Blown away by his admission, his hand gripped my throat before his lips crashed upon mine. I hadn't expected to come here and hear an admission like the one he had just given me, but I wasn't complaining. The taste of him on my lips had me moaning in satisfaction. His body pressed against mine as he kept me pinned to the wall.

"Are you sure you want this?" he whispered against my lips. "Are you sure you want the true side of me who is dark and fucked up but really good at his job? What you saw back there on earth… it was only one side of who I was. There is more to me than sunshine and rainbows. There is a darkness in me that can be uncontrollable."

I didn't need time to think about what he asked. The answer would always be, "Yes. A thousand times, yes."

Time seemed to stand still as our hunger for each other turned into a fury of torn clothing and touches. His hands roamed my body, gripping and grabbing as I pleaded with him to please me. To claim every inch of my body.

I wanted to feel the pain and pleasure he had created in me once before.

I wanted to know what it was like to be truly loved, to be worshiped.

Lifting me, he carried me. My legs wrapped around his waist as he took me back towards his bed. My body came in contact with the soft blankets upon his bed. Naked before him, he wasted no time in diving his face between my legs, his tongue finding the sensitive clit that had been begging for him since the last time he had me in this position.

"Oh, fuck," I cried out, my fingers wrapped within his hair as I rocked my hips, fucking his face until he had my toes curling. A scream ripped from my throat at the pure bliss that flowed over me.

Slowly standing, I watched him lick his lips as a wicked grin crossed his face. "My turn."

Grabbing my ankles, he flipped me over onto my stomach, my back arching as he grabbed my thighs, jerking me back until I was on all fours, my tight cunt on full display for him.

"This won't be like last time, Brina," he muttered, his hand running across the smooth round curves of my ass before he swatted it. The sting of his hit caused me to moan out in pleasure. "You like that, don't you?"

"Yes," I replied softly. "Please, stop teasing me."

His hand continued to slide across the bare surface of my ass, the ache in my core growing by the second. I needed him, but he was taking his time. Teasing me, taunting me in ways that I had never experienced.

The sound of clothing dropping to the floor made my heart beat with anticipation. The memory of how he had filled me, stretched me to my limits the last time he had taken me, flooded my mind. Slowly, his fingers slid up and down the slit of my wet pussy before I felt the head of his dick pressing against it gently.

He said it wasn't going to be like last time, but his actions had me confused.

Was he going to be easy, passionate? Or was he going to ravage me?

A hand in my hair jerked my head back, causing a squeak to escape my lips as he slowly slid himself in me, inch by inch. "You feel that? Feel me stretching you?"

I did feel it. Every single inch of his long, thick cock made its way inside me. Agonizingly slow. "What happened to this not being like last time?"

The sarcasm in my tone, laced with a seductive smile, caused him to laugh before he thrust himself with full force until he was hilted inside me. A cry left my lips as I tried to adjust, but it didn't last long before he held my hair tight and ravaged me over and over again.

The relentless aggression of his claim was overwhelming and though I had been fucked before, it was never like this.

Pulling me back, he spread my thighs. The angle in which he fucked me got deeper and deeper as he moved. His hand loosened from my hair as it slid down to my throat, his other hand coming up to cup my perky breast as his fingers rolled my erect nipple between them.

The sensation was enough to tip me over the top as I screamed, coming undone as he pounded into me faster and faster until finally he let loose a grunt, holding me close as he spilled within me.

My mind swirled with the vast array of emotions that consumed me. Staring at the window, the dark blanket of night having crossed the sky one thing became clear.

I couldn't leave without him.

CHAPTER
TWENTY-NINE

<u>**Tatum**</u>

I hadn't expected Brina to show up at my door looking for answers. At first I was annoyed that my sister would overstep boundaries in order to make things happen between Brina and me. Of course, I was head over heels for this girl. My heart slowly slipped into a bliss like state of happiness I hadn't expected.

My eyes slipped down to Brina's sleeping form, her chest rising and falling in a rhythmic pattern. Soft moonlight filtered through the window, casting a gentle glow upon her long hair that flowed out around her head like a halo up on the white pillows. Her thick black lashes lay against the smooth surface of her cheeks.

I had always wondered what my future would look like. What love would look like and in that moment, as I gazed upon her, I knew I couldn't let her go.

She had entered my life unexpectedly, weaving her way into the very fabric of my existence. Her laughter was like music, her touch electrifying. We had shared stolen glances and fleeting moments, overcame devastation and survived against all odds.

And now that I stood at the edge of this newfound love, I found myself confronted with the bitter reality of our circumstances.

She was leaving soon. Her fate was with Finnick in the Fae realm. My sister needed her guidance to help Pandora and Faeryn with their powers. However, the mere thought of her departure stirred a deep ache within me.

How could I lose her when I had only just discovered the depths of my feelings?

How could I let her slip through my fingers so easily?

A torrent of doubts and fears threatened to engulf me. Should I confess my love before she leaves, risk having my heart torn apart knowing that I can't keep her?

There was no real turning back after last night. No way that I could keep denying things. The way that Brina had curled up in my arms after we ravished each other spoke volumes to how we felt with one another.

In the face of my situation, I needed guidance, a voice of reason to help navigate the tumultuous sea of my emotions. Guidance from the only person who could possibly see reason and maybe change Brina's fate.

There had to be another way for us to get through every-thing.

A way that would allow us to be together.

One would think that it would be as simple as me going to the Fae realm with Brina, and perhaps once I could have. But I was a warrior of Asgard now. Sworn to protect the realm and guard its people from those who would seek to destroy it.

Making my way from the room, I strut through the halls towards her chambers. Each step echoed with the weight of my intentions, anticipation mingling with a sense of urgency that I couldn't ignore. I wasn't sure how I was going to start the conversation, but I knew that I had to make her listen.

There was no need for a guard to protect the halls. The entire building was enchanted and no one in their right mind would ever consider harming Cassie. At least not within this realm. She was respected and loved by all.

Raising my fist, I let out a heavy sigh as I knocked upon the white wooden door, waiting for her to answer. Her com-plaints of being woken in the middle of the night were sure to come my way, considering beauty rest was something she relished in.

"It better be fucking important!" I heard her yell from the other side of the door. The hinges allowed it to swing open freely as she stood before me in a white satin robe, her hair thrown up on top of her head with her eyes narrowed. "Tatum?"

"Hey, Cass. Can we talk?"

Glancing around, she rolled her eyes with a sigh before stepping aside to allow me to enter. My feet carried me across the threshold as I prepared myself for what I was about to say. "May it quick, Tate. But keep it down. Silas is sleeping."

Taking a deep breath, I summoned the strength to vocalize my inner turmoil. "Brina can't leave."

Her expression softened, a glimmer of empathy in her eyes as she nodded and made her way towards the small settee in her living room. "I had a feeling you would come to me about this."

"You did?" I replied with shock in my tone as I stared at her wide-eyed, slightly caught off guard by her admission. "But how—"

"I saw the day you brought her here how you felt about her," she replied, giving me a coy smile. "The eyes always betray the heart."

I hadn't realized that I had looked at Brina any sort of particular way, but my sister was definitely a very observant woman. And with her gifts, I should have known she would have known something.

She leaned forward, a thoughtful expression adorning her features. "You know the complexities of the realms, the obligations and duties that bind us. I know you love her and you want her to stay, but things aren't that easy, Tate. We need her there. We need her to help fix things before the girls rip apart the Celestial realms and all is lost. It's bigger than all of us."

The pain in her eyes showed the stress she felt over the situation. She was due to go back to the Fae realm some time ago, but until we could get Brina, she couldn't go. A small clue that I had overheard Pollux talking to Silas about back on earth a few years ago.

"I know, Cassie. But I can't...I can't just let her go...I only—"

"So don't," Sila's deep voice echoed from the doorway of their bedroom. Both Cassie and I turned our attention to his shirtless form leaned up against the door frame.

"What?"

"You heard me, don't let her go." Pushing off from the doorframe, he made his way towards where Cassie sat, standing behind her as he rested his hands on her shoulders, leaning down to kiss the top of her head.

"I'm not following."

His eyes slid up to meet mine before glancing down to Cassie. "I thought he was supposed to be the smart sibling."

Cassie swatted him with a smile as she laughed. "Oh, stop it. Tell him what you mean right now."

I didn't have a clue what they were on about, and the confused feeling that slithered its way through me didn't help to calm the anxiety that had been building up over the idea of losing her. However, Silas sighed, rolling his eyes and gazed at me.

"Brina is going to need a personal guard when she goes to the Fae realm. If you're interested..." he muttered, tilting his head from side to side. Joy surged from my chest as a smile grew on my face.

"I'll do it. I mean, if that's okay with you."

Cassie and Silas both looked at each other with a smile as she nodded in agreement. "Okay, okay. Who am I to stand in the way of love? However, just remember what the real task at hand is, Tate. We can't afford for her to get distracted."

"I understand," I replied with a nod. "But what are we going to do about her memories? She barely remembers anything, and in order for her to help...she has to know how to help."

I was stating facts and she knew it. There were so many factors that played into the family being whole again. So many factors in how Pandora and Faeryn would eventually get better. Which was crucial to everything.

My words seemed to touch them both as they continued to glance at each other. Cassie's hand laid upon Silas that rested on her shoulder, her fingers gripping it a little tighter before she sighed, turning her gaze to the floor. "Finn believes that he can help her with that. She resided in his realm for years, and there are still pieces of her there. Including the gateway to her father."

"Her father?"

Cassie nodded, her smile faltering. "Yes. Like I said to you before, there are a lot of factors to it all. Things you don't know...even things we don't know. We just have to have faith that when she remembers, that Brina can help us. That Balder will help us."

I hadn't realized just how dire everything had become since I had been in Asgard last. Back then my sister and her mates didn't seem to have a care in the world. They relished in the love they had. The children they bore. The life they had created. I never considered that perfection wouldn't last, especially for them.

But I guess even perfection has its flaws.

"I'll do my best to help her," I finally said, Silas nodding in agreement to my statement.

"Alright then, I think we should get some sleep. You both are leaving tomorrow."

Furrowing my brows in confusion, my lips parted to speak but Cassie beat me to it. "We were going to tell you both in the morning. Pandora had another episode. We got word from Finn a little while ago. Now that you're going with her, you can tell her."

Standing to my feet, I felt a weight lifted off my chest. My heart whole and my mind clear. There were tasks at hand, yes, but I was going to be with her. Brina and I would simply have to figure out everything else when we got to the Fae realm.

As long as she was by my side...she was all I needed in life.

CHAPTER
THIRTY

<u>Taylor</u>

When Tatum came crawling back into the room somewhere near dawn, I'd been wary of where he had gone. I had
awoken to an empty space in the bed next to me, and no word
as to where had disappeared. Though, when he had come
back and told me that I was to head off to the Fae realm in
the morning, my heart sank.

There were no words in regards to him coming with me or
anything. Not even a single word that explained his emotions
for me. Instead, I was greeted by the same man I had been
greeted by before and that was a triggering event. A sense of
rejection weighed heavily on me as I remained quiet, curled
up next to him wishing that morning would never come.

As he slept, I laid there. Staring at the ceiling thinking over
what was going to happen to me next. Thinking about what
I was going to do, and how I was going to make things work.

How was I supposed to help people when I couldn't even figure myself out?

The weight of the responsibilities they had placed upon me was overbearing. As if the entire world was resting on my shoulders. To help two children who didn't know me, in a place that I wasn't familiar with.

Tears filled the rim of my eyes as I slowly slipped from the bed making my way towards his bedroom window. The last thing I wanted was to wake him up, and as I stared out the window of Tatum's room I took in the sight of the sun slowly rising over the horizon.

"Brina?" His deep voice echoed from the space behind me. Quickly wiping my eyes, I forced a smile to my face, as I turned to face him.

"Hey," I replied, trying to keep my composure. "Did you finish everything you needed to get done last night? I'm sorry if I woke you."

"You're crying?"

It was a hesitant question, but one I was able to quickly shake off. "Just happy, that's all."

He stared at me for a moment before he stepped closer, his hands reaching out to lightly grip the sides of my arms before running up and down them in a comforting manner. "Are you sure? And yes, I did finish... If something is bothering you I want you to tell me."

Light laughter escaped me as I shook my head from side to side. "No, I'm fine. Honestly. I was just thinking about everything that had happened since you found me."

The uncertainty in his gaze as he furrowed them for a second before relaxing made me nervous. The last thing I wanted was to make me leaving difficult, and I didn't want to put any guilt on him either. It wasn't his fault that this was how things were meant to be.

We all had our part to play.

"Well, there will be plenty of time to dwell on the past later. For now, I need to get dressed. It's almost time for us to go. We have a portal to catch."

My ears perked up at the way he said 'we' as if he was coming with me. Though that couldn't be right, could it? "What do you mean we?"

A smile spread across his face as he pulled me in close, gently placing a kiss on my lips.

"I thought I told you this was forever and always," he replied, my heart beating rapidly out of my chest as the tears once again began to fall freely.

"You–you're coming with me?" I gasped, trying to hold back a sob that threatened to escape.

"Of course I am." He laughed. "Baby, where you go, I go. You're mine, and no one can take you from me."

His lips collided with mine in a deep passionate kiss. Our tongues explored each other as his hand slid up to entangle my hair. Knowing that he was going with me made things so much easier, and knowing that we were both immortal only made me feel more confident in his statement of forever and always.

Pulling from the kiss, he brushed his hand down against my cheek before kissing the tip of my nose. "We can explore this avenue of us later, Brina. Right now we have places to be, and the King of Tver waiting for us. And trust me when I say that my brother-in-law isn't a patient man. Lord knows how he has put up with my sister for all these years."

"Excuse me," a soft voice said from the door catching both of our attention. "I heard that."

Cassie stood before us in a long light-blue gown encrusted with gems. Her long hair was in curls half up on her head as the white silver leafed crown sat glittering on top. She looked so far different that her attire from our arrival, and even the crown seemed more earthly that the one she had been wearing prior.

"I'm sorry, dear sister. But you know it's true." Tatum laughed, a smile spreading over Cassie's lips as she shrugged her shoulders.

"Perhaps, but I know he will be excited to see me when I get there."

"Wait, you're going too?" I muttered, confused as to her coming. "I thought you had to rule here?"

Stepping forward she held out her hand to me, my eyes glancing up to Tatum, who nodded releasing me so that I could appease Cassie and take her hand. Turning, we slowly made our way out of Tatum's room, with him hot on our heels.

"Finn hasn't seen me in so long, and honestly...I miss being in the Fae realm. I wish that I could be with all my mates in the same place, but when you're a ruler, you must do what is best for your people. Even if you hate it."

I understood what she meant. Not about the ruling part or anything, but to have to do things even though you hate it. I had been in that position many times.

"I get it. But it must be hard leaving everyone."

She nodded slowly before glancing over her shoulder at Tatum. "You both are going to live an amazing life, Brina. But I want you to remember that the future of these realms, of the celestial plane, is in your hands. Even if you don't want to be in charge, in a way you are."

"No pressure then..." I murmured, my eyes finding Tatum who smiled chuckling to himself at my comment while Cassie seemed completely unfazed.

The moment we stepped back out into the lush green courtyard that I had first arrived in I found curiosity filling me over what the Kingdom of Tver would even look like. Would it be like the Fae kingdoms I had seen in movies back on earth? Would it be run down and dilapidated or perhaps they lived in homes high in the trees.

So many questions without answers made me eager to get to where we were going. Now with Tatum at my side, no longer did I feel hesitant or scared to go. Instead, I felt warmth and reassurance. Not to mention a future I had waited a lifetime for.

The shimmering cerulean blue light of the portal danced within the white marble frame that held it. The sun's rays peeking through the canopies of trees that surrounded the courtyard, the portals own little halo of gold that filled me with hope and wonder.

Before I had felt unease with going through the portal, with going to a new realm where again I would know no one. But now with Tatum going with me I felt stronger than ever. I felt safe, and knowing that I would have him to help and protect me made my heart swell with hope of the future.

Step by step, we made our way across the courtyard, Cassie, Silas, and Lucas stood with a few others I didn't know waited with smiles across their lips as we made our way towards the portal. I hadn't realized the moment would be a spectacular thing, but it seemed that they all wanted to bid us goodbye. As if this would be the last time we would see them.

Tatum stopped short of the portal in front of a woman with long platinum white hair. She looked young but her eyes, the same Cerulean blue as Tate's, held the secrets she seemed to hide. Secrets of a lifetime she lives, and the dangers that she had faced.

"Oh, my sweet baby boy," she muttered, her hands finding the side of his face as she brought him in for a hug, tears pricking the corner of her eyes. This was his mother…she looked to be no more than thirty, but that wouldn't have been possible.

"Mom," he grunted in her embrace as he slowly pulled away. "I want you to meet someone."

Her gaze slowly slid to me as a smile spread on Tatum's face. "This is Brina. Brina, this is my mother, Ivy."

"Thank you for taking care of him," she muttered. Tatum rolled his eyes behind her as if unable to believe perhaps that she was saying what she was. The entire situation caused the heat of embarrassment to rush over my cheeks as I cleared my throat.

"It's no problem…but I'm pretty sure it's he who has taken care of me."

Tatum didn't wait for his mother to continue the conversation as he nodded to the rest of the others and ushered me towards the portal. "It's time for us to go."

Taking a deep breath I nodded, my feet stepped towards the portal as he slowly began to disappear into it. His hand pulled me forward as I followed him into the unknown.

Towards a place I would be considered, a savior.

As we emerged from the portal, a kaleidoscope of colors as-saulted my senses. The landscape before us was a symphony of vibrant hues, with flowers of every shade imaginable carpeting the ground. As vines of green wrapped around every tree, pillar and stone of this place. Petals of blue, crimson, and gold danced in the gentle breeze, and even the air was heavy with the fragrance of blossoms, their sweet perfume intoxicating and soothing all at once.

"What is this place?" I gasped, my eyes turning towards Tatum who gazed at me with a grin across his lips.

"This is the Kingdom of Tver."

With his fingers still laced with mine, we walked hand in hand through the enchanted forests around the kingdom. The canopy above us forming a natural archway, as the sun's rays filtered through the open gaps leaving streams of light beaming towards the ground in various places.

The trees themselves seemed alive, their trunks adorned with intricate carvings as if the very essence of nature had intertwined with art, creating a wondrous blend of life and magic. A place where the impossible seemed to be possible.

"This place is beautiful," I muttered letting my fingers touch anything they could as we walked down the path. "It's like this entire place is alive."

"It is," Tatum quickly added. "I'm not entirely sure how it works, but the Fae have a special connection to their world. As if the world in which we stand right now is alive, working in unison with the Fae—both keeping each other alive."

My eyes glanced over to his as I stopped in my tracks trying to wrap my mind around what he was saying. "How is that even—"

"I don't know," he smirked. "You can ask Finn all about that though. He loves talking about this place almost as much as he loves talking about himself."

Rolling my eyes, I grinned at his comment. "You make him sound horrible when you say that."

"No, not horrid. Just annoying," he countered, the comment causing us both to break into a fit of laughter as we continued to venture further into the Fae forest.

The distant sound of cascading water reached my ears as the path ahead came to a large opening. My eyes eventually settled on a magnificent waterfall, its crystal-clear waters tumbling down the rocks into a large open pool below. An array of colors cast out into the sky, reflecting rainbow colored light into the air that seemed to disappear the moment the trickled droplets fell touching my skin.

It was there we found ourselves standing before the towering cliffs that housed the heart of Tver, the Castle in the sky perched on the highest peak, on the side of a cliff. It was a majestic structure of ivory and gold, adorned with delicate designs and stained glass windows that reflected the light of the sun, stars, and moon. It stood as a testament to the grandeur and power of the Fae.

A splendor that was more than breathtaking, creating a calmness that seemed to wash over me as if welcoming me home.

"Do you like it?" Tatum said softly, his arm wrapping around my waist as he pulled me close to him.

"It's beautiful," I gasped, letting it all soak in. "How could anyone want to live anywhere else when this place exists. I mean, I thought Asgard was gorgeous, but this...this far surpasses anything I could have ever imagined."

Leaning forward, he kissed the side of my head with a light-hearted chuckle as he held me close. "I'm glad you like it Brina. Welcome home."